"Are you worried?"

"About Beatrice? Yes."

"About everything," he responded.

Stella turned away, not wanting to look into his beautiful eyes. She knew what she'd see there. The same compassion and understanding she saw when he was questioning clients or reassuring a victim. He had a way of making people open up to him.

She didn't like opening up to anyone. She didn't like feeling vulnerable. She *hated* being on the receiving end of pity.

"You need to trust me to handle things the way they need to be handled," Chance said. "You're not the only one who's worried. I don't want to see anything happen to you or your grandmother, and I can't do my job effectively with one hand tied behind my back."

"I'm not tying anything. I'm setting boundaries."

"Boundaries that are going to get you killed."

Aside from her faith and her family, there's not much **Shirlee McCoy** enjoys more than a good book! When she's not teaching or chauffeuring her five kids, she can usually be found plotting her next Love Inspired Suspense story or wandering around the beautiful Inland Northwest in search of inspiration. Shirlee loves to hear from readers. If you have time, drop her a line at shirlee@shirleemccoy.com.

Books by Shirlee McCoy

Love Inspired Suspense

Mission: Rescue

Protective Instincts
Her Christmas Guardian
Exit Strategy
Deadly Christmas Secrets
Mystery Child
The Christmas Target

Rookie K-9 Unit

Secrets and Lies

Capitol K-9 Unit

Protection Detail
Capitol K-9 Unit Christmas
"Protecting Virginia"

Heroes for Hire

Running for Cover
Running Scared
Running Blind
Lone Defender
Private Eye Protector
Undercover Bodyguard
Navy SEAL Rescuer
Fugitive
Defender for Hire

Visit the Author Profile page at Harlequin.com for more titles.

THE CHRISTMAS TARGET

SHIRLEE MCCOY

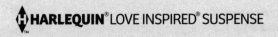
HARLEQUIN® LOVE INSPIRED® SUSPENSE

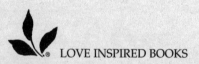

LOVE INSPIRED BOOKS

ISBN-13: 978-0-373-44776-3

The Christmas Target

Copyright © 2016 by Shirlee McCoy

www.Harlequin.com

Printed in U.S.A.

In your unfailing love
you will lead the people you have redeemed.
In your strength you will guide them to your holy dwelling.
—Exodus 15:13

To Marge Garrison. My favorite breakfast buddy.
I sure miss you!

ONE

Stella Silverstone woke like she often did—bathed in sweat, heart beating frantically, her body screaming for her to run or fight.

She did neither.

She wasn't on a hostage rescue mission in the middle of Vietnam. She wasn't in Egypt, walking through the slums, searching for a missing child. She was just outside of Boonsboro, Maryland, caring for her grandmother because her grandfather was gone.

He'd been eighty-three when he'd taken his last breath. Stella couldn't say that his life had ended too soon, but she would have happily traded a few years of hers to have him back. Henry Radcliff had been a keeper. That's what Stella's grandmother had said at the funeral. She was right. Henry had been a great guy. A wonderful husband, a loving father, a protective and caring grandfather.

Now he was gone, and Stella had to take his place in Beatrice's rambling old Victorian, helping her grandmother do everyday chores that suddenly seemed to be too much for her—laundry, cooking, dry mopping the hardwood floor, paying bills and sending thank-you cards. A year ago, Beatrice could have handled all of that and more. Now she seemed confused, frustrated and a little scared.

That scared Stella.

Which was probably why she'd woken in a panic.

That and the fact that Christmas was only three weeks away.

Her least favorite day of the year.

She shivered, glancing at the glowing numbers on the bedside alarm clock. Nearly 5:00 a.m. Her boss, Chance Miller, and a few members of HEART would be converging on the house in a couple of hours. The hostage extraction and rescue team had bimonthly meetings at headquarters. Meeting outside of that secure environment went against protocol. The team coming to Boonsboro should have been out of the question. Stella had tried to argue with the plan. She could have easily found someone to watch Beatrice for the day while she made the three-hour trip to DC.

Chance had insisted that they do things his way. He knew what he wanted, and he always went after it. When Stella had protested, he'd told her that he wasn't interested in her opinion. Then he'd said goodbye and hung up. If he'd been anyone else, Stella would have seen that as rude, but Chance was never rude. He was almost never wrong, and Stella had been just tired and distraught enough to let things go his way without a fight.

He hadn't gloated, hadn't pointed out that he'd finally won one of their many arguments. He'd just emailed notes for the meeting, told her that he'd update her on a few potential clients and asked if there was anything she needed him to bring when he came.

She'd wanted to be angry with him for insisting on doing things his way. Mostly because she'd spent the past year trying really hard to convince herself she and Chance were past tense. Their brief relationship had burned out faster than a candle in a rainstorm, and she didn't want to relight it.

At least, that's what she kept telling herself.

For a while, that had been really easy to believe. The two had been butting heads for nearly as long as they'd known each other, but there was something very real beneath the constant bickering, some indefinable thing that always made her want to jump to Chance's defense, make certain he was okay, watch his back. She knew he felt the same about her. He proved it every time he did something like this—planning a meeting around her schedule and her life.

Truth? Chance wanted to bring the meeting to Boonsboro because he was worried about her. He'd never say it. He didn't have to. Stella knew it.

Just like she knew that she wanted him there, because she needed someone she could lean on. For just a minute.

She was tired.

Beyond tired.

Her grandfather's death from a sudden heart attack had been shocking, but finding out that her grandmother had been diagnosed with Alzheimer's had pulled the rug out from under every plan Stella had ever made.

Three years. That's how long her grandparents had known about the diagnosis. Three years that they'd kept it secret because they hadn't wanted Stella to give up the job she loved. That's what Beatrice's best friend, Maggie, had said. Stella had wanted to know about the medicine she'd found in the bathroom cabinets, the post-it note reminders plastered all over the house, the forgetfulness and confusion that Beatrice seemed to be suffering from.

Of course, the nurse in Stella had already known what all those things meant. She just hadn't wanted to believe it. Maggie and Beatrice had been friends since elementary school, and Stella had known that her grandmother's friend would have the answers she needed.

She just hadn't expected those answers to hurt so much.

And they did.

It hurt to know that Nana was losing her memories. It hurt to know that the vibrant, cheerful woman who'd raised Stella was going to become a shell of the person she'd once been.

It also hurt to hear that her grandparents had thought she loved and valued her job more than she loved and valued them. But then, why wouldn't they think that? She'd spent so much time away that she hadn't seen the signs and symptoms of Alzheimer's until her grandfather was gone.

It was a regret she'd live with for the rest of her life. If she'd spoken to them on the phone more than once a week, asked the right questions, delved a little deeper into their lives, maybe she would have realized the truth long before Granddad's death. Then she could have told Henry that she'd give up her work at HEART for Beatrice.

So far, it hadn't come to that.

She *had* given up her apartment in DC, moved back to the huge old Victorian that Beatrice had inherited from her parents decades ago. Stella had even tried to resign from HEART. Working as a member of one of the most well-respected hostage rescue teams in the world took time and energy that she needed to devote to her grandmother.

Chance had refused to accept her resignation. She'd been working for the company since he and his brother Jackson founded it, and he had told her that the team couldn't run without her. That was an exaggeration. They both knew it, but Stella loved her work. She didn't want to give it up. She wasn't even sure who she would be without it. She'd built her entire life around HEART.

Now she was trying to rebuild it around her grandmother.

Chance had made it very clear that he'd support her in any way he could. He'd assigned her paperwork and research, report writing and about six other things that were menial compared to the high-risk jobs she'd been taking before Granddad's death.

Just until you and your grandmother get back on your feet, and you will, Stella. It's just going to take some time.

She could still hear his voice, see the compassion in his dark blue eyes. He'd come to the funeral. Of course he had. Chance always did the right thing. Always.

Stella wasn't sure why that made her feel resentful. Maybe because she often found herself doing the wrong thing. Or maybe because he'd done so many right things the few times they'd dated, and she'd still managed to chase him away.

She stood, her toes curling as her feet hit cold wood.

No sense lying in bed fretting about things she couldn't change. She'd be better off making a pot of coffee and finishing up the last of the three hundred thank-you notes she'd been writing out since Granddad's funeral. Keep busy. It had been her motto for as long as she could remember. Especially this time of year.

Wind rattled the old wooden panes and whistled beneath the eaves, the sounds nearly covering another more subtle one. Floorboards creaking? A door opening?

Beatrice?

Had she woken already?

Stella stepped into the dark hall, not bothering with the light. She'd walked through the drafty house thousands of times during the years she'd lived there. She'd memorized the wide hallway, the landing, the stairs and the banister. She knew how many doors were on each side of the hallway and which ones creaked when they opened.

Beatrice slept in the room at the far end of the hall, and Stella went there, knocking on the thick wood door. When Beatrice didn't answer, she turned the old crystal knob and stepped into the room.

"Nana?" she whispered into the darkness, shivering as cold air seeped through her flannel pajamas.

Cold air?

She flicked on the light, her heart stopping when she saw the empty bed, the billowing curtains.

She yanked back gauzy white fabric, nearly sagging with relief when she saw the window screen still in place, the mesh flecked with fat snowflakes.

"Nana!" Stella called, throwing open the closet door. Just in case. Her grandmother had gotten lost walking through the house recently. One day she hadn't been able to find the kitchen. Another day, she'd stood in the hallway, confused about which room she slept in.

"Nana!" Stella yelled it this time, the name echoing through the house as she ran out of the room. She could hear the panic in her voice, could feel it thrumming through her blood. She never panicked. Ever. But she felt frantic, terrified.

"Beatrice!" She yanked open the linen closet, the door to the spare room, the bathroom door.

She thought she heard a faint response. Maybe from the kitchen at the back of the house.

She barreled down the stairs and into the large foyer.

The front door was closed, the bolt locked. Just the way she'd left it. She could feel cold air wafting through the hallway, though, and she spun on her heel, sprinting into the kitchen.

The back door yawned open, the porch beyond it covered with a thin layer of snow. She thought she could see footprints pressed into the vivid white, and she shoved her feet into old galoshes, ran outside.

There! Just like she'd thought. Footprints tracking across the porch and down into the yard. She should have called for help. The practical part of her—the part that was trained as a trauma nurse, who knew protocol and statistics and the necessity of using the brain instead of the heart during stressful times—understood that. The other part, the part that only cared about finding Beatrice as quickly as possible, was calculating just how far an eighty-one-year-old with Alzheimer's could go in the time it took to make a phone call and get the police involved.

Pretty far.

Especially when going just a couple of hundred yards would mean entering thousands of acres of forest.

"Nana!" Stella screamed, sure that she saw a shadow moving at the back edge of the yard. The woods began there—deep and thick, butting up against the state forest, crisscrossed with tributaries of the Patuxent. An easy place to get lost and hurt. Especially if a person was elderly and frail, and probably not dressed for the weather.

Stella ran toward the trees, hoping the shadow she'd seen had been her grandmother. *Praying*, because that's what Beatrice would have wanted her to do. It's what Henry would have expected her to do. Granddad had been a retired preacher. After watching his son take over the pulpit, he'd planned to spend time going on mission trips, traveling with his wife, enjoying the fruit of a life well lived. He'd ended up raising Stella instead.

He'd never complained about that.

He'd never accused God of unfairness, never said he'd been given a rough shake.

He'd believed that everything happened for a reason, and that good could be found in the most trying circumstance if a person took the time to look for it. He'd been an eternal optimist, because he'd believed that God's will trumped all else.

Stella was a pessimist. Mostly because she believed the same thing.

She reached the edge of the yard and found footprints in the snow there, nearly covered by a fresh dusting of white. She should have grabbed her cell phone on the way out. She should have grabbed a coat. A flashlight. Warmer clothes.

Rookie mistakes, but she was committed now. She couldn't let Beatrice get any farther ahead. She plunged into the thick foliage, branches catching on her hair and tugging at her skin. She thought she heard a car engine, was sure she heard voices coming from the front yard.

No one should be anywhere near the house. They were too far from town for random strangers to show up and none of Beatrice's friends would be out at this time of morning.

Stella would have checked things out, but she had one goal—finding her grandmother.

"Nana!" she shouted.

To her left, branches snapped, and she turned, certain Beatrice would be there.

"What are you doing out—"

Someone lunged from the darkness. Not an eighty-one-year-old; this person moved fast, flying toward Stella, swinging something at her head.

She had a second to react, one heartbeat to duck. The blow glanced off her temple, sent her reeling. She fell into a tree, slid to the ground, but all she could think about was Beatrice. Out in the woods. Near the creek.

She scrambled up, blocked another blow. Dizzy from the first, disoriented, fighting because she'd been trained to do it. Blood in her eyes, sliding down her cheeks, blinding her in the swirling snow. *Nana, Nana, Nana*, chanting through her head.

She landed one blow, then another. She felt something behind her—some*one*. No time to duck, just searing pain, and she was falling into darkness.

* * *

Something was wrong. Chance Miller felt it the way he felt the frigid air and the falling snow. He rounded the side of the huge old house, Simon Welsh at his side, Boone Anderson still at the front door, ringing the bell. For the tenth time.

There was no way Stella had slept through the noise.

She didn't sleep. Not much. When she did, she slept lightly, every noise waking her. He'd learned that during long flights across the Pacific Ocean and long journeys in foreign countries. She also didn't like being surprised. Ever.

And his early morning visit?

It was a surprise.

Stella was expecting him later in the day, but he'd been worried about the coming snowstorm. If it hit the way the meteorologists were predicting, driving later in the morning might have been a problem. He'd decided to leave DC before the snow began to fall. If he got stuck in Boonsboro, no problem. But he'd been worried enough about Stella that he didn't want to postpone seeing her.

She'd been too quiet lately, and quiet wasn't her style. Usually she was loud and decisive, more than willing to explain exactly how she thought things should go.

As a matter of fact, he'd expected her to yank open the door as soon as the bell rang and ream him out for arriving before he was scheduled.

She hadn't, and he figured that could only mean one thing.

Trouble.

It whispered on the cold wind, splashing down in the heavy flakes that fell on his cheeks and neck. Light streamed out from a door that yawned open, the yellowy glow splashing across the back porch. He could see the interior of the house, the bright kitchen, the white cupboards and old wood floor.

He didn't bother walking inside.

No way had Stella left the door open. Not intentionally. Not unless there'd been an emergency that had sent her running from the house.

He eyed the snow-coated ground, crouching to study what looked like boot prints. Not large, and he'd guess a woman had been wearing them. There was another print a few inches away, a different type of shoe. Something without tread and nearly covered by a fresh layer of snow.

"What'd you find?" Simon asked.

"Footprints. Two sets. Heading toward the woods."

"Stella's?"

"I think so, and maybe her grandmother's."

"Looks like she might have left this way," Simon said, moving up the porch stairs and peering inside. "You want me to check things out, or do you want to split up and search the yard and woods?"

The newest member of the team, Simon had worked for SWAT in Houston before joining HEART. He had keen instincts and the kind of work ethic Chance appreciated. He also had the same driving need to reunite families that everyone on the team possessed.

He didn't know Stella, though.

Not well, and he couldn't know just how serious this situation was becoming. Stella didn't leave doors open. She didn't take chances. She played by the rules, and she expected other people to do the same. Something had sent her running, and he was pretty sure he knew what it was.

Who it was.

Her grandmother.

"If Stella were inside, she'd be out on the porch giving us a piece of her mind. She's left for some reason, and I'm worried that reason might be her grandmother."

"She's prone to wandering?"

"She has Alzheimer's, so it's a good possibility." Chance took a penlight from his pocket, flashing it into the yard. Snow fell in sheets now, layering the ground in a thick blanket of white. Soon it would cover whatever tracks the women had left. Once that happened, finding them would be nearly impossible.

Please, God, help us find them before then, he prayed silently as he moved across the yard, his light bouncing over white snow and sprigs of winter-dry grass.

A few yards out, it glanced off what looked like another footprint. Chance moved toward it, studying the ground more carefully, finding another footprint and another one.

"This way," he said, not bothering to see if Simon was following. He would be. They knew how to run a mission. No reason to go over all the variables, discuss a plan. With the temperature below freezing, there was no time to waste.

Frantic people made errors in judgment. Like leaving a house in a snowstorm without letting anyone know they were going. Not that Chance would ever use the word *frantic* to describe Stella. She was one of the most clearheaded people he knew.

If she'd panicked, there had to be a good reason. Her grandmother wandering around in the snow fit the bill. He'd met Beatrice twice. She'd seemed sweet, kind and very fragile.

If she was out in the cold, she'd need medical attention. If the snow continued to fall and her footprints were covered, he and his team would need help searching the woods that surrounded the property.

So, maybe, Stella wasn't the only one who'd panicked.

Maybe he'd been panicking, too. Acting on emotion rather than clear thinking. Not a good way to proceed.

"Change in plans," he said, stopping short and motioning for Simon to do the same. "Call 911. Let's get the local authorities in on this."

"You want me to call it in as a missing person?"

"Yes. I'm going to see how far I can follow the tracks. Get Boone and follow after you've made the call." He jogged across the yard.

The boot prints were faint but obvious. Stella had left the house recently. He wasn't sure about Beatrice. He'd only seen one print that he thought was hers, and it had been left earlier. He hoped not too much earlier. He and Stella had their differences, but he only ever wanted the best for her. The best thing for her right now would be for her grandmother to be okay.

She'd be devastated if something happened to Beatrice, and Chance would be devastated for her. Stella was special. She had depth and character and just enough stubborn determination to keep Chance on his toes. Of all the women he'd dated, she was the only one he hadn't wanted to walk away from.

He'd done it because it was what *she* had wanted.

Or, at least, what she'd said she'd wanted.

There were plenty of days when he regretted letting her go. He never mentioned it, and she never asked, but he'd have rekindled their relationship if she'd given any indication that she wanted to.

Pride goeth before the fall.

How many times had his father said that?

Too many to count, but Chance was still too proud to crawl back to a woman who'd sent him away. That was the truth. Ugly as it was. So, they were stuck in a pattern of butting heads and arguing and caring about each other a little more than coworkers probably should.

A little more?

A lot more.

"Stella!" he called, pushing through thick foliage.

Someone had been there ahead of him. Branches were broken, the pine boughs cleared of snow. The thick tree canopy prevented snow from reaching the ground, but he could see depressions in the needles that covered the forest floor.

He followed them, stepping through a thicket and walking onto what looked like a deer trail. Narrow, but clear of brambles and bushes, it would be the path of least resistance for anything or anyone wandering through the woods.

"Stella!" he called again. "Beatrice!" he added. He could imagine the elderly woman wandering through here, finding the open path and heading in whatever direction she thought would lead her home.

A soft whistle echoed through the darkness.

Boone and Simon, moving into the trees behind him. He didn't slow down. They'd find their own way.

Cold wind bit through his heavy coat, and he wondered if Stella had dressed for the weather. If she'd left in a panic, would she have bothered?

He jogged along the path, the dark morning beginning to lighten around him. The sun would rise soon, warming the chilled air. But soon might be too late, and he felt the pressure of that, the knowledge of it, thrumming through his blood.

Somewhere ahead, water burbled across rocks and earth.

A deep creek or river?

He thought he heard movement and ducked under a pine bough, nearly sliding down an embankment that led to the creek he'd been hearing.

He stopped at the edge of the precipice, flashing his light down to the dark water below. A shallow tributary littered with large rocks and fallen branches, it looked easy enough to cross once a person got down to it.

He aimed the beam of light toward the bank, searching for footprints or some other sign that Beatrice or Stella had been there.

Just at the edge of the water, a pink shoe sat abandoned on a rock.

Not Stella's. She never wore pink.

"Beatrice!" he called. He needed to phone Simon and give him the coordinates. They could begin their search from there, spread out along the banks of the creek and work a grid pattern until they found the missing women.

"Beatrice!" he yelled again.

Someone dove from the trees, slamming into him with enough force to send them both flying. He twisted, his arms locked around his assailant as he fell over the edge of the precipice and tumbled to the creek below.

TWO

Stella had to take her attacker down. She knew that, and it was all she knew. Everything else—the darkness, the cold, the blood—they were secondary to the need to survive and to find Beatrice.

She'd been a fool, though.

She should have waited longer. Instead, she'd rushed out when she'd heard the man calling Beatrice's name. Now she was trapped in a vice-like grip, tumbling down, unable to stop the momentum.

Unable to free herself.

She fought the arms clamped around her waist. Blood was still seeping from the cut on her temple and a deeper wound on the back of her head. Sick, dizzy, confused—she knew the symptoms of a concussion, and she knew the damage could be even worse than that. Brain bleed. Fractured skull. She'd been hit hard enough to be knocked unconscious. She needed medical help, but she needed to protect Beatrice more.

She slammed her palm into her attacker's jaw, water seeping through her flannel pajamas. The creek? Had she come that far?

Had her grandmother?

Fear shot through her, adrenaline giving strength to her muscles. She slammed her fist into a rock-hard stomach.

"Enough!" a man growled, his forearm pressing against her throat, his body holding her in place.

"Not hardly!" she gasped, bucking against his hold.

Suddenly he was gone, air filling her lungs, icy water lapping at her shoulders and legs as she gasped for breath.

She thought maybe she'd imagined him, that the head injury was causing hallucinations, or that she was hypothermic and delirious. Then a hand cupped her jaw, and she was looking into Chance Miller's face.

He looked as shocked as she felt.

"You're in DC," she said, surprised at how slurred the words sounded, how difficult they were to get out.

"No," he said, his arm slipping under her back as he lifted her out of the water. "I'm here."

She thought she heard a tremor in his voice, but that wasn't like Chance. He always held it together, always had himself under control.

"Always perfect," she murmured.

"What?" he asked, and she realized they were moving, that somehow he was carrying her up the bank and away from the creek. Snow still fell. She could feel it melting on the crown of her head, sliding into the cut on her temple. None of it hurt. Not really. She just felt numb and scared. Not for herself. For her grandmother.

She had to concentrate, to stay focused on the mission. That was the only way to achieve success. She'd learned that, or maybe she'd always known it, but it had kept her alive in more than one tough situation.

"Put me down." She shoved at Chance's chest. "I have to find my grandmother."

"Boone and Simon will find her. You need medical help."

"What I need," she said, forcing every word to be clear and precise, "is to find my grandmother. Until I do that, I'm not accepting help from anyone."

"We've already called the local authorities. They should be here soon. They can conduct the search while an ambulance transports you to the hospital."

"I'll just transport myself back. So how about we make this easy and do things my way for a change?"

"We do things your way plenty. This time, we're not." He meant it. She could hear it in his voice. She could feel it in the firmness of his grip as he carried her through the snowy woods.

And he was right.

She knew he was right.

She needed medical attention.

She needed help.

But she couldn't go to the hospital. Not while Beatrice was still lost in the woods.

"Chance, I can't leave without her. I can't." Her voice broke—that's how scared she was, how worried. Her grandmother was out in the cold, and someone was out there with her. Someone who'd attacked Stella.

More than one person?

She thought so, thought she'd been hit from behind, but she couldn't quite grasp the memory.

Chance muttered something, then set her on her feet, his hands on her elbows as she found her balance. It took longer than she wanted, the world spinning and whirling, the falling snow making her dizzy. Her stomach heaved, and she swallowed hard. No way was she going to puke. If she did, it would be over. Chance would carry her back to the house and send her off in an ambulance.

Focus on the mission.

"Something is going on," she said, afraid if she didn't get the words out, she'd forget them. "Someone is out here."

"*We're* out here," he said, turning on a penlight and

flashing it across the creek bed. Something pink sat near a rock a few yards away.

"Not just us. Someone attacked me."

He stilled, the light holding steady on that pink thing, his gaze suddenly on Stella. "Who?"

"I don't know. He came out of nowhere. One person. Maybe two."

"Did you see his face?"

"No."

"Did he speak? Say anything to you?"

"No."

"How long ago was that?" He strode to the object, lifted it.

Her grandmother's slipper.

Stella had bought them for Beatrice three Christmases ago, knowing her grandmother would love the faux fur and sparkly bows. Funny that she could remember that, but she had no idea how long she'd been out in the snow.

"That's my grandmother's," she said, that thickness back in her throat again.

"Stella," he said, the calmness in his voice the exact opposite of the panic she felt, "how long have you been out here?"

"I don't know. Maybe fifteen minutes."

"Were you unconscious at any point?" His gaze drifted from her eyes to the bleeding cut on her head.

"Yes."

"So it could have been longer than fifteen minutes?"

"Yes. Now how about we stop talking about it and start looking?"

"Okay," he said. Just that, but she felt better hearing it.

Because of all the people she knew, Chance was the one she trusted most to get things done.

His light illuminated the shadowy bank at the far side of the creek. The sun hadn't risen yet, but the forest was tinged with grayish light. No sign of Beatrice that Stella could see, but, then, her eyes didn't seem to be working well, everything shifting in and out of focus.

In the distance, sirens wailed.

Help coming too late?

Please, God. Not too late.

The prayer was there. Just on the edge of her thoughts, and she tried to follow it with more words, more pleas, but her mind was spinning, her thoughts scattering. Her stomach heaved, and she was on her knees retching into dusty snow and pine needles.

"It's okay." Chance crouched beside her, his cool palm on the back of her neck, his coat dropping around her shoulders. She felt him tense, knew he'd realized that she had another head wound. Double the potential for severe injury, and he'd be calculating the risk to her versus the risk of leaving the creek while Beatrice was still wandering around in the snow.

If they went back to the house, Beatrice would probably die before anyone found her.

The temperature was below freezing, the snow falling faster and heavier. And Beatrice's slipper had been in the creek. Which meant she'd been in the creek, too.

"I want you to wait here," Chance said quietly. "I've already texted our coordinates to Boone and Simon. They'll be here soon. One of them will wait with you until the medics get here."

Not a question.

Not a suggestion.

He really thought that she was going to wait at the edge of the creek while Beatrice wandered through the snowy forest.

She struggled to her feet, following him as he stepped across the burbling water. He didn't tell her to go back. He didn't waste time or energy arguing with her. It was one of the things she'd always liked about Chance—he didn't spend time fighting battles when he had wars to win.

"There's a print there." His light settled on an impression in the muddy bank. "Let's see how many more we can find."

He started walking parallel to the creek, and she followed, her heart beating hollowly in her ears, her legs weak, her body still numb.

Voices carried through the woods, men and women calling out to one another. A search party forming, but Stella could only think about taking one step after another, following the tracks that Chance's light kept finding. Bare feet pressed into the muddy earth. Bare feet in below-freezing temperatures.

Stella was shivering uncontrollably, and she had Chance's coat. Beatrice probably had nothing but her cotton nightgown and the gauzy robe she put on each morning when she got out of bed.

She tasted salt on her lips and realized hot tears were mixing with icy snow. She never cried around other people. Ever. She was crying now, because she'd already lost her grandfather, and she wasn't sure she could bear losing her grandmother, too.

She swiped the tears away, tried to clear the fog from her mind at the same time. She had to think. She had to imagine being in Beatrice's shoes, walking outside, making her way to the creek. Had someone been with her? Maybe the person who'd attacked Stella?

Or had she gone off by herself? Maybe reliving some long-ago day? A trip to the creek with Henry, a picnic in the moonlight? Had some memory sent her wandering?

Had she—

"There!" Chance shouted, the word sending adrenaline coursing through Stella again.

He sprinted forward, and she followed, tripping over

roots and rocks, trying desperately to see what he was seeing.

There! At the edge of the creek! White against the dark ground and glistening water. Gauzy fabric, a thin pale leg peeking out from it.

"Nana!" Stella sprinted forward, grabbing her grandmother's hand as Chance lifted her lifeless body from the water.

They'd always been a good team.

Always.

Worst-case scenario, best-case, didn't matter. Chance and Stella knew how to move in sync. He wasn't sure that was going to save Beatrice. Stella's grandmother was as limp as a rag doll, her skin icy cold. No respiration. Pulse—thready and weak.

"She's not breathing," he said, laying Beatrice on flat ground and checking her airway.

"Nana?" Stella said, giving her grandmother's shoulder a gentle shake. "Can you hear me?"

Beatrice remained silent, her face bone-white.

"Let Boone know where we are so the medics can find us more quickly. She needs help now. Not ten minutes from now." Stella wrapped Beatrice in his coat and began CPR. No chest compressions. Just rescue breaths that made Beatrice's chest rise and fall.

He made the call quickly, his gaze on the trees that edged close to the creek. The morning had gone silent, nothing moving in the shadowy pre-dawn light. It wasn't a safe stillness. It wasn't a good silence. Something was off—the air subtly charged, the shadows seeming to shift and undulate. He pulled his Glock from the holster, stepping away from Stella and her grandmother. Behind him, voices drifted through the trees—the medics moving toward the creek as he moved away from it.

Stella didn't ask him where he was going or what he was doing. She was either so focused on her grandmother she hadn't noticed or she sensed what he did—someone watching.

The woods had lightened imperceptibly, black trees now brown-gray, white snow flecked with green pine needles and fallen leaves.

He used his penlight anyway, training it into the heart of the forest, flicking it across thick tree trunks and winter-brown bushes. He didn't want to go too far. Even with help close at hand, he was worried about leaving Stella and her grandmother. Both were in bad shape. Stella, at her best, could take down almost any well-trained fighter. But she wasn't at her best. Not even close.

He reached the top of a shallow embankment, the snow thicker there, the trees sparser. His light bounced across a fallen log, illuminating a hint of bright pink that peeked out from behind it.

The other slipper. He didn't move closer. He'd spent years in Afghanistan and Iraq, working as part of one of the top ranger teams in the army. He didn't talk about those days, but he'd lived them. They'd been the best preparation in the world for the kind of work he did with HEART.

Always cautious.

Always meticulous.

Always weighing risk versus benefit.

Until there was nothing to do but act, and then he'd do whatever was necessary to get out alive with his comrades.

The slipper?

It looked like one of the dozens of booby traps he'd seen just sitting out in the open, waiting for someone to pick it up. He flashed the light to the left and right of it, searching for wires or leads. Nothing. Not that he'd really expected there to be anything. Booby traps didn't happen all that often in the good old USA, but he was paranoid, and he believed what Stella had said. *Someone's out here*.

Her words had explained the gash on her temple, the blood that stained the collar of her pajama top and matted her dark red hair. She needed the medics almost as badly as her grandmother did. Maybe just as badly. He'd seen people die of head injuries like hers. He knew how dangerous they could be. If she'd been a different kind of person, he'd have carried her back to her grandmother's house and made sure she was in an ambulance heading for the hospital, but Stella knew her own mind, she made her own decisions. He'd have done the same if he were in her position—insist on being part of the search. So, he'd let her call the shots.

But he wasn't going to let her get hurt again.

Someone's out here.

Yeah. She was definitely right about that.

He crouched near the slipper, his light trained on the ground beyond it. He studied the layer of pine needles and dead leaves, found what he thought were depressions in the surface. He followed the trail with his light, surprised to see what looked like a path through the trees. Not a deer trail this time. It looked man-made, the ground clear of shrubs and undergrowth.

Stella's attacker had gone that way. He was certain of that. He was also certain that whoever it was wouldn't be returning. Not now. Too many people crisscrossing the woods, too many lights flashing above the creek. Only a fool would risk capture by sticking around.

He saved the coordinates of the trail and holstered his Glock. He'd pass the information on to the team, let them figure out where the path led. Once he made sure Stella and Beatrice were safe, he'd return. By that time, local law enforcement would have already scoured the area, but he'd take a look anyway. It was what he did. Double-check. Look where others might not. Sometimes, a second or third or fourth pair of eyes would uncover something that no one else had.

If the police came up empty, Chance was going to make sure he didn't. Right now, he had a lot more questions than answers, and he didn't like it. Had this been a random act? An opportunistic crime? Or had it been planned?

Stella had worked a lot of missions. She'd made a lot of friends, and she'd made a few enemies. It was possible one of them had followed her to Boonsboro.

He frowned, turning back toward the creek.

She'd have been an easier target in DC. She lived alone there, in an apartment on the top floor of an old brown-stone. He'd been to her place twice, and he'd lectured her both times. Not enough security. The doors were flimsy. The locks were a joke.

She'd told him to mind his own business, but that was Stella. She liked to do things her way. When it really mattered, though, she knew how to follow protocol and work as part of a team.

He moved toward the creek, retracing his steps, following the sound of voices and the flashes of lights through the forest. He thought he heard Stella, her voice about as familiar as his own. They'd known each other for a long time. Long enough to know each other well.

And to care about each other deeply.

He'd seen her crying while they searched for Beatrice. He wasn't going to mention it. Not to her. Not to anyone on the team. Stella was indestructible and unflappable. At least, that's what she wanted everyone to think.

The air changed, and he knew he wasn't alone, that someone was just out of sight, hidden by the heavy boughs of a giant conifer. He didn't pull his firearm. Anyone who wanted to take a shot at him would have already done it.

A shadow separated itself from the trees, the gray edge of dawn highlighting red hair and a tall, narrow frame.

Despite his height, Boone Anderson moved quietly, his footfalls silent on the pine needles. "Find anything?" he asked.

"One of Beatrice's slippers and a path through the woods."

"We going to follow it?"

"You and Simon can. Let the local PD know what you're doing and where you're heading."

"You'll be at the hospital?"

"Someone has to be."

"Stella can usually take care of herself."

"She's in bad shape. I don't think she'll be doing much of anything for a while."

"How bad?" Boone cut to the chase. No extra questions. No speculating. He was a straight shooter. He did his job and he did it well, but his heart was with his family—his wife, his new baby, the daughter he'd lost years ago and had recently been reunited with.

"Probably a lot worse than she's going to admit. A pretty deep gash to the temple and one on the back of her head."

"And she probably thinks she's going to be up running a marathon tomorrow."

True. That was Stella. To a T.

"Where's Simon?"

"Sent him down to the creek to see what the ruckus was about. Looked like the medics were carrying a gurney in. I'm assuming they've got to carry someone out. The grandmother?"

"We found her in the creek. She wasn't breathing."

"Pulse?"

"Yeah."

"Then she's alive, and we're going to pray she stays that

way." Boone pulled out his cell phone, texted something, then slid it back in his pocket. "I told Simon you were on your way. You go do what you need to do for Stella and her grandmother. We'll keep you in the loop, and we'll play nice with the local PD."

"You'd better. I don't think you'll like prison food."

Boone snorted, pulling something out of his pocket and holding it up for Chance to see.

A bag of homemade cookies.

Typical of Boone. The guy never stopped eating.

Any other time, Chance might have smiled.

Right at that moment, all he could do was think about the tears that had been sliding down Stella's cheeks. He'd never seen her cry. Not on the worst missions. Not when she'd been exhausted or tired or injured. Not when things had seemed hopeless or the person they'd been looking for had been found too late.

Not even at her grandfather's funeral.

Never.

Not once.

Because Stella didn't cry.

Except that she did, and he'd seen it, and he didn't think he'd ever forget that.

Boone opened the bag and took out a cookie. Unflappable. Just like always. He'd done what he'd been asked to do, and he'd keep doing it, but first, he'd eat.

"I always come prepared. Tonight, it's a dozen homemade chocolate chip cookies," he said. "I'll share, but only because my wife told me I have to."

"You can tell her that you tried, but I'm not in the mood for cookies."

"Worrying won't change anything. You know that, right?" Boone bit into the cookie, his gaze as direct as his comment.

"That won't stop me from doing it. Keep your nose

clean, Boone. I'm heading out." Chance jogged back to the creek, every nerve in his body on high alert. He hadn't expected trouble. He'd found it.

Now he was going to deal with it.

A dozen people were standing near the creek—police, park rangers, paramedics. Simon stood next to Stella, his hand on her shoulder, not holding her up but pretty close to it.

He met Chance's eyes, mouthed, *She's done*.

"I am not," Stella bit out, her body shaking beneath a blanket someone had tossed over her shoulders. "Done."

"That's a matter of opinion," Simon countered as paramedics lifted Beatrice onto a backboard. She'd been swaddled in blankets and had an IV in her hand, but she was breathing, an oxygen mask covering her mouth and nose. That was an improvement, and it gave Chance hope that she might recover.

"My opinion is the only one that matters," Stella muttered, but she didn't seem interested in the argument. She was watching as the medics strapped Beatrice to the board and lifted her.

"Careful," she warned, as if the team needed to be reminded.

They ignored her.

Which was surprising since she had blood dripping down the side of her face and more of it seeping from beneath her hair. She was also pale as paper, her skin completely leached of color. Chance would have thought every available medic would be hovering around, cleaning her wounds and getting her ready to be transported. She must have refused treatment, insisted that the attention be given to her grandmother.

Now her grandmother was on the move, and Stella looked like she planned to follow.

"I don't think so," he said, grabbing her arm.

"You don't think what?" she asked, trying to pull away.

He didn't have to put much effort into keeping that from happening. Which concerned him. A lot. "That you're going to walk back to the house."

"I don't think you have a choice in the matter."

"Sure I do. Just like I had a choice when I didn't drag your butt back to the house. I let you decide then. This time, I decide."

"This is not the time to go macho on me, Chance," she growled. "I'm in no mood."

"And I'm in no mood scrape you off the forest floor. So, how about we stop arguing and get this done? Your grandmother needs to get to the hospital, and you're slowing things down."

She pressed her lips together, and didn't say another word as an EMT urged her to sit down, then cleaned both wounds.

"This one looks okay," the EMT said, pressing gauze to Stella's temple, "but you're probably going to need stitches to close the other one."

"I've had worse," Stella muttered, brushing the young woman's hands away and holding the gauze in place herself. "Has the ambulance left with my grandmother?"

"Yes," the EMT admitted. "She's in a very critical state and needed to be transported immediately. We've called another one for you."

"There's no need for another ambulance. I'll drive myself. My grandmother might be confused, and I really need to be there with her."

If she hadn't been dead serious, Chance would have laughed.

"Ma'am," the EMT said before Chance could, "you're in no condition to drive."

Stella must have agreed, because she eyed Chance with a look he'd seen many times before. It was the one that said she needed him, but she didn't want to. The one that said she couldn't do it alone, but wished she could.

He understood the look and the feelings behind it.

"I'll give you a ride," he offered before she could decide whether or not to ask, and she smiled. A real smile that softened her face and made her look sweet and young and vulnerable. It surprised him, because she hadn't directed a smile like that at him since they'd broken up. He'd forgotten how powerful it was; forgotten how it made his pulse race and his heart pound.

"Thanks. I really appreciate it."

"You know I'd do anything for you, Stella," he said, and meant it.

Her smile faded, and she was just staring into his eyes, looking wounded and tired and a little too fragile for Chance's peace of mind.

Finally, she shrugged. "You're the first guy to ever say that to me."

Odd considering that she'd been married for years. Her husband had died serving his country, and she'd mentioned once or twice just how proud she'd been of him.

That was about as much information as she'd given.

Even when Chance had asked.

Even when they were dating.

"Then you haven't had the right guys in your life," he responded, keeping his tone light.

She wasn't herself.

That was obvious. He didn't want her to regret their conversation or be embarrassed by it.

He took her arm, helped her to her feet. "Do you have a spare key to the house? Boone and Simon might need to get inside."

"I left the door open."

"There are police everywhere. Someone might have closed it."

"There's probably a key in the flower box outside the kitchen window. If you want to look for it, I can—"

"No."

"You don't even know what I was going to say."

"Whatever it was, the answer is still no. We're getting out of these woods, and I'm driving you straight to the hospital. No stops for anything."

"You're awfully bossy when I'm hurt," she muttered. There was no heat in her words and no real complaint.

"Awfully worried," he corrected, taking her elbow and helping her up the embankment.

"Don't be. I'm fine."

"You always are. Until you aren't, and then I have to ride to the rescue," he replied, baiting her the way he had a hundred times before. He knew how she'd react. Her back would go up, her chin would lift, and she'd march to the house like she hadn't been knocked unconscious and nearly frozen.

It almost worked out that way.

"I've rescued you more times than you've ever rescued me," she said.

Just like he knew she would.

Then she shrugged away from his hold, marching forward with just enough energy to convince him she might actually be okay.

They made it through the trees and out into the yard, white snow swirling through the grayish light. He could see how pale she was, see how much she was trembling. She was cold or in shock or both, and he had about two seconds to realize that baiting her hadn't worked out the way he'd wanted before her steps faltered.

Just a little hitch in her stride, a soft sigh that he barely heard, and she was crumbling to the ground so quickly Chance barely had time to catch her.

THREE

She was in the car again, the beautiful book her grand-parents had given her for Christmas in her hands.

"Don't touch it," she snapped at Eva. Her sister was only four, and she liked to ruin things—paintings, draw-ings, schoolwork. Eva was always scribbling on them.

"Be kind," her mother admonished, turning in her seat and smiling, her beautiful red hair curled, a pretty green Christmas ribbon woven through it.

Matching hairstyles. Stella and Eva had ribbons, too. Even tiny little Bailey had a bow in her fuzzy hair.

That kind of made Stella proud.

She loved her family. Even Eva.

"Okay, you can touch it," she said, and her sister smiled with Daddy's dark brown eyes, and then the world exploded in heat and flames and horrible screams.

She was screaming, too. Screaming and screaming, her throat raw, her head pounding. Someone calling her name over and over again.

Stella woke with a start, bathed in sweat, pain throb-bing somewhere so deep inside she wasn't sure where it came from or how to get rid of it.

"Shhhhh," someone said, hands brushing across her cheeks, wiping away the tears that always came with the Christmas dream.

Christmas *nightmare*.

She took a deep, shuddering breath, realized she was hooked to something. An IV?

Was she in the hospital?

Suddenly the fog cleared, and she knew where she was, what had happened.

"Nana!" She shoved aside blankets, tried to get to her feet, but those hands—the warm, rough ones that had wiped her tears—were on her shoulders, holding her still.

"Slow down, Stella."

Chance.

She should have known, should have recognized the hands, the deep voice.

"Where's my grandmother?" she asked.

"In ICU. Stable." He was leaning over her, his dress shirt unbuttoned at the neck, his tie dangling loose, his gaze steady and focused.

He was the most handsome man she'd ever seen, the kindest man she'd ever known. She tried really hard not to think about that when they were working together.

Right now, they weren't working.

For a moment, it was just the two of them, looking into each other's eyes, everything else flying away. If she let herself, she could drift into sleep again, let herself relax knowing that Chance was there. She wouldn't let herself. Her grandmother needed her.

Stable. That's what Chance had said.

It was a good word, but she wanted more. Like *conscious, talking. Fine.*

"I need to see her."

"You're in no shape to go anywhere or see anyone."

"I'm seeing you," she retorted, sitting up a little too quickly. Pain jolted through her skull, and she would have closed her eyes if she hadn't been afraid she'd be in the nightmare again.

"You're funny, Stella. Even when your skull is cracked open," he responded, his hand on her back. He smelled like pine needles and snow, and she realized that his shirt was damp, his hair mussed.

Not perfect Chance anymore.

Except that he was—the way he was supporting her weight, looking into her eyes, teasing her because he probably knew she needed the distraction. All of it was perfect, and that made it really hard to remember all the reasons why she and Chance hadn't worked out.

All the reasons?

She could only really think of one—she'd been a coward, too afraid of being disappointed to risk her heart again.

She shoved the covers off, turned so her feet were dangling over the side of the bed. She was wearing a hospital gown. Of course. Her feet bare, her legs speckled with mud and crisscrossed with scratches. She could have died out in the woods. If Chance hadn't shown up, she probably would have.

If she'd died, what would have happened to Beatrice? She knew the answer. Beatrice would have died, too.

It didn't make sense.

The town she'd grown up in was quiet and cozy. Movie theaters, shopping centers, a bowling alley and an ice-skating rink. The nice-sized hospital she was in had been built in the sixties and had a level one trauma center. People hiked and biked and ran, and they generally died of old age or disease. Not murder.

She frowned.

Was that what all this had been? Attempted murder? It didn't seem possible. Not in Boonsboro. Trouble didn't happen there. At least, not the kind that took people's lives. Not usually. Not often. One of the worst things that had ever happened in town was the accident that had

killed Stella's family. It had been the worst tragedy since
the old Harman house had gone up in flames at the turn
of the nineteenth century. Four children died in the fire.
Two adults. The grave plot was still tended by someone
in the family, but Stella had never paid much attention to
it. She'd had her own family to mourn, her own graves
to tend.

She shoved the thought and the memory away, pushed
against the mattress and tried to stand. Failed.

"Need some help?" Chance slid his arm around her
waist, and she was up on her feet before she realized she
was moving.

The room was moving, too, spinning around her, making her sick and woozy. Maybe Chance was right. She
wasn't in any shape to go anywhere.

In for a penny. In for a pound.

That's what her grandfather had always said.

She was already standing. She might as well try to
walk.

She took a step, realized she was clutching something.
Chance's belt, her fingers digging into smooth leather,
her shoulder pressing into his side. He was tall and solid,
not an ounce of fat on his lean, hard body. He could hold
her weight easily, but she tried to ease back, stand on her
own two feet, because it's what she'd always done. Even
when she was married. Even when she should have been
able to rely on someone else, she'd taken care of herself,
handled her own business, stood alone more than she'd
stood beside Daniel.

"There is no way you're going to make it. You know
that, right?" Chance said.

"Sure I am." She grabbed hold of the IV pole and took a
step to prove him wrong. Took another one to prove to herself that she could do it. Her legs wobbled, but she didn't

fall. She made it to the door and put her hand on the jamb for support, the hospital gown slipping from one shoulder.

Chance hitched it back into place, and she knew his fingers must be grazing the scars that stretched from her collarbone to her shoulder blade. She didn't feel his touch. The scars were too thick for that, the skin too damaged.

His gaze dropped to the spot where his fingers had been, and she knew he wanted to ask. Not how she'd gotten them. He knew the answer to that. He did background checks on every HEART operative. No, he wouldn't ask how she'd gotten them. He'd ask if they hurt, if there was something he could do to take the pain away, if the memories were as difficult to ignore as the thick webbed flesh.

He'd asked those things before, and he'd told her how beautiful she was. Not despite the scars. Because of them. They made her who she was, and he wanted to know more about how they defined her.

She hadn't answered the questions, because getting close to someone meant being hurt when they left. She'd been hurt enough for one lifetime, and she didn't want to be hurt again. If that made her a coward, so be it.

"How about I get you a wheelchair?" Chance said, his breath tickling the hair near her temple, his hands on her shoulders. Somehow, he was in front of her, blocking the doorway, and she wasn't even sure how it had happened.

She was worse off than she'd thought.

But she still needed to see Beatrice. For both of their sakes.

"Okay," she agreed, because she didn't know how she'd make it to the ICU any other way.

"And how about you sit and wait while I do it? I don't want you to fall while I'm gone." He was moving her backward, his hands still on her shoulders.

She could have stood her ground. But her legs were

shaky, and when the back of them hit the bed, she would have fallen if he hadn't been holding her.

"Careful." He helped her sit, his tie brushing her cheek as he reached for the blanket and pulled it around her shoulders. Yellow. That's what color the tie was. With a handprint turkey right in the center of it. Only a guy like Chance could wear a tie like that and still lead the most prestigious hostage rescue team in North America.

"Nice tie," she murmured.

He crouched so they were eye to eye, smiled the easy smile she'd noticed the first day they'd met. The one that spoke of confidence, kindness and strength.

"A gift from my niece for Thanksgiving. I promised I'd wear it to my next meeting."

"And you always keep your promises."

For a moment, he just stared into her eyes. She could see flecks of silver in the dark blue irises. He had the thickest, longest lashes she'd ever seen, and when they'd dated, she'd told him that.

"I try," he finally said. "I'll be back in a minute. Don't leave the room without me. They still haven't found the guy who attacked you, and I don't want to take chances. Boone is outside the ICU, making sure your grandmother is protected. You're my assignment."

"I'm your *what*?" she asked, but he'd already straightened and was heading out the door, pretending that he hadn't heard.

If she'd had the energy, she would have followed him into the hall and told him just how likely it was that she was going to be anyone's assignment. She'd been taking care of herself for years. Daniel had been part of an elite Special Forces unit and had been gone more than he'd been home during their marriage. When he was home, he'd been distant and unapproachable. She'd loved him, but their three-year marriage had been tough. If she was honest with herself, she'd admit that she wasn't sure if it would have survived.

She'd wanted it to, but she and Daniel had both had their demons. They'd only ever fought them alone. That didn't make for a good partnership. She knew that now. Maybe because she'd spent the last few years fighting beside and with Chance.

"Not the time," she muttered. She had more important things to think about. Like the fact that the police hadn't found the man who'd attacked her.

Men?

She still wasn't certain.

If she had her cell phone, she'd call the local sheriff's department for an update, but she'd left it at the house. There was a phone beside the bed and she picked up the receiver, tried to remember the sheriff's number. Her mind was blank, her thoughts muddled. She dropped the phone back into the cradle and grabbed her pajamas from a chair near the window. Someone had folded them neatly. Her galoshes sat beneath the chair, side by side.

Chance?

She could picture him folding the clothes, setting the boots in place. Everything precise and meticulous.

She walked into the bathroom. It took a second to pull the IV from her arm, took a couple of minutes to wrangle herself into the pajamas. Her hands were shaky, her movements sluggish, but she didn't want to be running from the bad guys in a too-big hospital grown.

Running?

She'd be fortunate if she could crawl.

Damp flannel clung to her legs and arms as she splashed cold water onto her face and tried to get her brain to function again. No dice. She was still woozy and off balance. A concussion? Had to be. She lifted the gauze that covered her temple, eyeing the wound in the mirror. The bump was huge and several shades of green and purple. No stitches. Just a long gash that looked like it had been glued shut.

She had a bandage on the back of her head, too. She didn't bother trying to see. She felt sick enough from the effort she'd already put in.

Someone knocked on the bathroom door. One hard, quick rap that made her jump.

"Hold on," she called, grabbing the handle and pulling open the door.

Chance was there.

He didn't look happy.

As a matter of fact, he looked pretty unhappy.

"Why am I not surprised?" he asked, his gaze dropping to her pajamas and then jumping to the IV pole.

"You'd have done the same," she responded.

"True, but that doesn't mean I approve. You have a concussion. You're supposed to be resting."

"I'll rest better after I see my grandmother."

"You won't rest. You'll be out hunting down your attacker unless someone is there to stop you." He took her arm, the gentleness of his touch belying the irritation in his eyes.

"No one would dare try," she responded, jabbing at him like she always did. Usually, he jabbed right back, but this time he just shook his head.

"How about we not test that theory, Stella? Because I have better things to do with my time than babysit someone who won't follow the rules."

"I hope you're not talking about me."

"I told you. You're my assignment. Or rather, keeping you safe is."

"Since when?"

"Since about two nanoseconds after you collapsed on

your way to my car. Sit." He gestured to the wheelchair that was near the bathroom door.

"I'm not a dog."

"Trust me. I am very, *very* aware of that."

She was suddenly self-conscious in her wet pajamas. But this was Chance. He'd seen her looking a lot better, and he'd seen her looking a whole lot worse. They'd crossed a river together once, emerging on the other side soaked to the skin and shivering with cold.

Yeah.

This was Chance. There was nothing he didn't know about her and no situation he hadn't seen her in.

She blushed anyway, dropping into the wheelchair so quickly that pain exploded through her head.

Her eyes teared but she didn't close them.

If Chance realized how much pain she was in, he'd insist that she get back into bed. Truth? She didn't think she'd have the energy to fight him. She felt so tired, she thought she could close her eyes and sleep forever.

"Maybe this isn't a good idea," Chance muttered, grabbing the blanket and tossing it over her legs.

"Did you ever think it was?"

"No," he replied, pushing the chair out into the hallway.

There was too much noise there, too many lights—her head spun with all of it. She had to see Beatrice, though, and then she needed to talk to the sheriff. She didn't have time to give in to pain or to lie in bed feeling sorry for herself.

Someone had attacked her.

She had to hold on to that, had to keep it in the front of her mind so that she stayed focused on the goal—find the guy, figure out his agenda.

Maybe he'd been a vagrant, wandering through the woods, startled by a woman suddenly appearing.

Maybe, but it didn't feel right. The entire thing felt too coincidental.

"Have you spoken with the sheriff?" she asked as Chance wheeled her into the elevator. "I know you said that they didn't find the perp, but I'm wondering if they found anything else."

"They traced the guy to an old logging road that runs through the woods behind your property. They've cast tread marks that he probably left behind. Other than that, they've come up empty."

"That's not the news I wanted."

"I know."

"Maybe he was a vagrant." She tossed the theory out, because Chance was as likely to see the strengths and weaknesses in it as she was. More likely. He wasn't concussed, and he wasn't sitting in a wheelchair with bandages on his head.

"Someone just moving through who was squatting out in the woods and panicked when you showed up?"

"It's possible, right?"

"Anything is possible, Stell. That doesn't make it likely. Right now, I don't have enough information to speculate, but if I were going to guess, I'd guess the attack wasn't random." The elevator door opened, and he wheeled her out.

"You've got a reason for that. Care to explain?"

"You said there were two perpetrators."

"Possibly two," she corrected.

"I've never known you to make a mistake. If you say there might have been two, it's because there probably were. If that's the case, a squatter who panicked seems unlikely."

"Squatters don't always live alone."

"It sounds like you want to believe the attack was random."

"Don't you?"

"I want to believe the truth. For right now, I'm keeping an open mind. Sheriff Brighton is still on the scene with half a dozen men. He said he'll stop by the hospital when he's finished. We'll know more then."

"Did they—"

"Stella, this isn't your case. It's not your mission. You are the victim, and you've got to let the local police handle the investigation."

"I plan to, but I'd like to talk to Cooper—"

"You and the sheriff are on a first-name basis?"

"We went to school together. I want to talk to him."

"You'll have plenty of opportunities to do that. After you rest. The doctor said three or four days in bed."

She snorted, then wished she hadn't. Pain shot through her skull and her ears rang.

Up ahead, double wide doors opened into the ICU unit. Several nurses sat at a desk there.

Stella scanned their faces, trying to see if she knew any of them. She volunteered at the hospital once a week. It kept her sane, helped her focus on something besides her own problems and her own sorrow. She probably knew half the nurses who worked there, but her vision was too blurry, everything dancing and swaying as she tried to focus.

"Stella!" one of them cried, rushing around the counter and running toward her.

Not a nurse. A volunteer.

The uniform came into focus. The name tag. The pretty brunette. Karen Woods. A nursing student at the local college and the person who stayed with Beatrice when Stella had to be away from home for more than a few hours.

She should have recognized her immediately.

She probably would have if the world had been standing still.

"Are you okay?" Karen had reached her side and was leaning toward her, the smell of her perfume mixing with antiseptic and floor cleaner and making Stella's head swim. "I was working on the pediatric floor and heard Beatrice had been admitted. What happened?"

"She—"

"Tell you what," Chance interrupted. "How about we hash it all out after Stella sees her grandmother?"

Karen frowned. "Of course. I was just so relieved to see her, I wasn't thinking. I was going to visit Beatrice, but there's a guy outside the door who says she can't have visitors. I told the nurses, but they said you want him there, Stella."

"I do," she responded, the words echoing hollowly in her ears. She felt light-headed and sick, and she wanted to grab Chance's hand, hold on tight so she didn't float away.

"Why? Are you worried that Beatrice wandered off? Do you think she's getting worse? I heard she left the house without a coat or shoes." Karen's words came in quick staccato beats that slammed into Stella's head and made her want to close her eyes.

She liked Karen.

The young woman was smart and helpful, and she'd been wonderful with Beatrice, but right at the moment, Stella wanted to tell her to go away.

She needed to think.

She couldn't do that with someone talking nonstop, asking questions she had no answers for.

"Karen," she began, but Chance's hand settled on her shoulder, his thumb sliding against her neck, and she lost what she was going to say. Felt herself just give it over to him, because he was there, and he could handle it and she was more than willing to let him.

She'd think about what that meant later.

When she wasn't so tired, so scared, so concerned.

"It seems like you've heard a lot of information in a very short amount of time," he said, his tone conversational and light.

Chance waited for the young woman to respond. Karen Woods. That's what her name tag said. He'd seen her before. Probably at the funeral. He remembered the brown hair and the big smile. If she remembered him, she didn't let on. Just offered a quick shrug.

"The entire hospital is buzzing with the news. Beatrice and her husband helped fund the pediatric wing. They're a big deal here."

Stella looked like she was trying to think of a suitable response, her brow furrowed as if she couldn't quite come up with the words.

Chance figured no response was necessary.

"Big deal or not, Beatrice isn't to have any visitors unless they're approved by the police or by Stella. You know that, right?"

"I'm not stupid."

"It's not about stupidity. It's about knowledge. Were you informed?"

"Yes."

"Then you'll understand that Stella is going to have to say goodbye for now. She wants to see her grandmother, and—"

"I'm not invited?" Karen smiled, but there was something hard in her eyes. "No need to hit me over the head with it."

"I'm not trying to. I just want to make certain we're all clear on the rules."

"Because you're so big on them," Stella murmured, and he smiled.

She was right.

But that was why they got along so well.

"Only when they matter. We'll see you when we come out," he said, pushing the chair past Karen.

He wasn't asking permission, and he didn't wait for a response. He wanted Stella to see her grandmother, and then he wanted her back in the hospital bed.

She was two shades too pale, red hair falling lank against her neck and cheeks. Her hand trembled as she tucked a strand behind her ear, and he wanted to turn the chair around and go straight back to her room.

He knew Stella, though.

She'd find her way back.

With or without him.

Family was everything.

She'd told him that dozens of times when they were on a mission together. She'd proven how much she meant it when she'd tried to give up her job to take care of her grandmother. Chance hadn't been able to let her go. She was too valuable a team member. And the team was its own sort of family.

He pushed her through the hallway of the ICU, Karen following along behind despite the fact that he'd made it really clear that she wasn't going in Beatrice's room. She looked well-meaning enough, but there was a glimmer in her dark eyes that bothered him. A little bit of excitement that shouldn't be there. He'd seen it before—some otherwise harmless person determined to get the juiciest bit of gossip and spread it to the four corners of the earth.

He imagined she had a nice little group of friends that she'd love to give all the details to. She'd be the star, have her five minutes of fame because she'd brushed shoulders with a couple of people who'd almost died.

She wasn't getting any information from him, and he doubted Stella would share anything. Not if she was thinking clearly.

Several closed doors lined the hall. Boone was in front

of one, sitting in a chair, his legs stretched out, the bag
of cookies in his hand. He'd eaten half. Chance was surprised he hadn't eaten them all.

"I see you finally made it up here," he said, his gaze on
Stella. "You look like death warmed over, Silverstone."

"Thanks."

"It wasn't a compliment. It was a hint that you should go
back to bed." His gaze shifted to Karen, and he frowned.
"Are you here to try to kick me out again, Karen?" he
asked, and the young woman blushed.

"I wasn't trying to kick you out. I just didn't understand why you were sitting here."

"I told you why," he said with typical Boone patience.
The guy was almost never bothered by anything or anyone. "Next thing I knew, hospital security was trying to
kick me to the curb."

"I know, but—"

"Karen," Stella cut in. "I appreciate you wanting to
visit with Beatrice. Tomorrow will probably be a better day."

It was a dismissal, and Karen seemed to get it.

Finally.

She patted Stella's shoulder. "Of course. If you need
anything, you know how to reach me. I have classes tomorrow and Friday, but I'm free Saturday and Sunday if
you want me to clean the house and do some shopping."

"I'll let you know."

"I can also stay here with Beatrice, if you need me to."

"I think we've got everything under control." The
words were kind and a lot more patient than was typical of Stella.

"Okay. Great. Good. Like I said, you know how to
reach me." Karen hurried off, and Stella sighed.

"She means well," she said, and Chance wasn't sure if

the words were a reminder to herself or information for him and Boone.

"It didn't feel like it when security was trying to strong-arm me out of here," Boone muttered, pulling a cookie from the bag. "I nearly lost these babies fighting for my right to stay."

"I'm sorry she called security on you, Boone."

"Not your fault." He stood, brushed crumbs from his lap. "If you two are going to be in there for a few minutes, I'm going to run and get coffee. Maybe see how the cafeteria food looks. You want anything?"

"Juice. Orange. And a black coffee," Chance responded. He'd drink the coffee, and hopefully he could convince Stella to drink the juice. She still looked shaky, and that worried him. She also looked thinner than she had the last time he'd seen her. A month ago. Maybe a little longer than that. She'd come to DC to pick up a computer system that she could use for work.

She'd said she was fine, that her grandmother was fine, that things were going well. He'd heard a lot that she hadn't said. Or maybe he'd just assumed that things weren't as easy as she claimed, that life wasn't quite as fine as she was making it out to be, because that's the way Stella was.

She didn't need help.

She didn't want it.

Everything was always okay and fine and good.

When a guy got too close, when he asked too many questions, she backed off and walked away.

He'd watched it happen over and over again.

He'd experienced it firsthand.

She wasn't the kind of woman who wanted more than an easy and light relationship. She didn't want to share her soul. That's what she'd told him on their last date when he'd asked about her family, about the accident that had taken them from her.

I don't go out to dinner with a guy so I can share my soul with him. Sharing a meal is good enough.

He'd told her that he only ever wanted to be with someone who could share every part of herself.

That was it.

A bad ending to a story that should have had a great one. He and Stella had a lot in common. They clicked in a way he'd never clicked with any other woman. He could have made a life with her, but he wasn't going to insist. He wasn't going to beg. He wasn't going to do anything but give her exactly what she'd said she wanted.

"You want anything, Stella?" Boone asked, calling her by her first name. Something he almost never did.

That seemed to shake her out of whatever stupor she'd fallen into.

She frowned, locking the brake on the wheelchair and getting to her feet. "Just to see my grandmother."

"You go do that. I won't be long," Boone continued, meeting Chance's eyes. "I'll call Simon and let him know what's going on here."

"See if he's got anything new from the local police."

"And ask when the sheriff is going to get here. I want to speak with him." Stella took a wobbly step toward the door.

"Take it easy," Chance said, taking her arm before she could face-plant into the door.

"If I take it any easier, I'll be prone in a bed."

"That's where you should be."

"Not yet." She opened the door and stepped into the quiet room.

A heart monitor beeped a steady rhythm, and the soft hiss of an oxygen machine filled the room. From what Chance could see, Beatrice's vitals were normal. Or close to it. Her oxygen level was low, but the mask over her face should help with that.

Stella leaned over the bed rail and kissed her grandmother's cheek. "Nana?"

When Beatrice didn't respond, Stella lifted her hand, studied the gnarled joints and short nails. "She used to love having her nails done."

"Did she?" Chance pulled a chair over to the bed and nudged Stella into it.

"She thought it made a woman feel feminine. She always wanted me to have mine done, too, but I was never a girly girl, and I hated it. One year, we had matching nails for Christmas. Hers were green with little red Christmas trees. Mine were red with little green Christmas trees. Christmas morning, I realized she'd bought us matching outfits, too. Long red skirts and white blouses with high collars. I think she was going for a Victorian vibe."

"How old were you?"

"Fifteen."

"I guess the Victorian theme didn't go over well with you."

"No." She smiled at the memory. "But I wore the outfit to church anyway. Becky Snyder never did let me live that down. I heard about it every other day for my entire high school career."

"I'm surprised you didn't shut Becky down." That was another thing Chance had watched happen over and over again. Stella knew how to put people in their places and how to keep them there. She also knew how to lift them up when they needed it, offer support when no one else could. It made her fantastic at her job, and it drew people to her. No matter how many times she tried to push them away.

"Why would I? I never cared what anyone else thought. Beatrice was happy. That made me happy."

"I'm sure your grandmother wouldn't have been happy if she'd known you were being teased."

"She knew. We used to laugh about how ridiculous Becky was for bringing up something *so last year*. And about how silly she was to think that someone who'd survived what I had would be bothered by her opinion." She smiled at the memory.

"Your grandmother was a smart lady."

Maybe she'd heard the past tense. Maybe she'd realized just how much of herself she'd just shared.

Whatever the case, her smile faded, her gaze shifting to Beatrice's face. "I hope she weathers this. She's already frail, and her memory isn't good. Sometimes older people don't recover from—"

A siren split the air, the sound shrieking through the silent ICU.

Stella jumped from the chair, swayed.

Chance just managed to grab her waist, holding her upright as her grandmother bolted into a sitting position.

"What's happening?" she cried, her voice muffled by the oxygen mask.

Good question.

Chance wanted an answer as badly as she did.

"I don't know, but I plan to find out. Stay here," he said, looking straight into Stella's eyes.

She didn't argue.

She wouldn't leave her grandmother's side. That was one blessing. For once, he absolutely knew that Stella would stay exactly where he'd left her.

He sprinted from the room, the siren still screaming as he raced down the hall to the nurses' station.

FOUR

The siren cut off as abruptly as it had begun.

Stella listened to the sudden silence.

No. Not silence. There were sounds. Subtle noises mixing with the beep and hiss of machines.

She could hear voices. Nurses and doctors talking, their excited chatter drifting in from the hall. They weren't moving patients. That was good news, but it didn't make her feel better. It didn't make her feel confident that things were okay.

She didn't like this.

She didn't like it at all.

"Is there a fire?" Beatrice asked, her voice hoarse, her face pale.

"Probably just a drill," Stella assured her and tried to reassure herself.

No one would be foolish enough to launch an attack in the hospital.

Would they?

"Are you sure? Because where there's sirens, there's bread."

"Where there's smoke, there's fire, Nana, but there's no smoke. Sometimes hospitals check their equipment. Just to make sure everything is working." Sometimes, but not often. Not with sirens that could scare heart patients into cardiac arrest.

"I hope you're right, dear. After last night…"

"You remember last night?"

"How could I not? People shouldn't throw rocks at glass. It can cause all kinds of problems."

"Rocks at glass?" She was listening with half an ear, most of her attention on the door. She wasn't sure what she expected. Maybe some masked gunman rushing in, ready to take Beatrice out.

Or take her out.

She had a lot more enemies than her grandmother.

As a matter of fact, she'd be surprised if Beatrice had any enemies at all. Stella? She'd earned plenty of them. In her line of work, that went with the territory.

"I had to tell him to leave, but he told me that he had a message from Henry, and I had to come down and get it."

"Who had a message from Henry?" Now she was focused, now she was really listening, and she *still* wasn't sure what she was hearing.

"The man with the rocks. The one who woke me up."

"Nana, there was no man with rocks."

But maybe there was.

Maybe that's what had woken Beatrice and sent her out into the storm.

Beatrice pulled the oxygen mask away from her face, her blue eyes blazing with irritation. "Of course there was, Stella. I may be losing my marbles, but I don't imagine things. Yet." She let the mask drop back, and her eyes closed.

She was either tired of talking or tired of trying to explain what had happened. Either way, Stella let her be. She had bigger things to worry about and more pressing matters to attend to. She'd figure out the window and the rocks and the man with the message after she figured out why the siren had gone off.

She walked to the door, her legs like noodles, her knees weak. She hated to admit it, but Chance had been right when he'd said she'd be better off in bed. The injuries to her head weren't the worst she'd had, but they sure didn't feel good, and they sure didn't make her steady on her feet.

The room seemed to tilt as she moved, the walls swaying. She needed Chance's steadying hand, and she wasn't sure how she felt about that.

She hadn't ever wanted to need him, but she thought that she always had. From the moment she'd met him, she'd known he was going to be trouble, that he was going to ask for a lot more than she wanted to give. She'd joined his team anyway. She'd dated him.

She'd sent him packing.

And she'd regretted it.

She still regretted it.

She frowned and opened the door, her hand clammy, her skin damp with sweat. She felt sick and she felt scared, and she didn't like either.

The corridor was empty. No nurses running to prep patients for evacuation. No security officers rushing through looking for trouble. Just the soft beep of machinery, the ⁚iet hiss of ventilators. Everything seemed to be func-tɩ ꞏing normally.

ꞏt the alarm had gone off. That meant something waꞁ ꞏormal.

Roɯ. ꞏt glass.

The words ran through her head as she took a step toward the nurses' station.

Rocks at glass.

She thought about Beatrice's room, the curtains billowing from the open window, the dusting of snow beneath it.

Had there been footprints?

Had she looked?

Her sluggish brain clicked along, the connections harder to make because her mind was functioning at super-slow speed.

Rocks at glass.

Someone had been throwing something at the window and woken Beatrice. That was the easiest explanation for what had happened. A few rocks, a little noise, and Beatrice had woken and gone to the window.

And had been given a message that she couldn't ignore? One that had sent her outside into the snow? Why would anyone do that to a harmless elderly woman?

A nurse stepped through the double doors. Male. Tall. A mask covering his face, his hair a dark shade of brown that didn't look natural. Too monotone. Too dull.

Her brain was still chugging along slowly, but she knew. Even before he moved. Even before she realized he was heading in her direction.

Trouble.

It was written in the lines of his body—tense and rigid.

She didn't question the instinct to move back, to put herself in a position to guard the doorway to Beatrice's room.

His gaze was on the floor, trained away from her with such determination that she knew he felt her gaze. He moved past, and she almost believed that was it, that she'd imagined the shiver of unease, the feeling that he wasn't what he seemed.

Then he was on her, turning so quickly she almost didn't see the movement. A knife flashed in the light, and if she hadn't been so well-trained, if her muscles hadn't been conditioned to react before her brain, he'd have taken her out with one swipe of the blade.

She blocked the attack, shoved him back, tried to rip at

the mask on his face. She was seeing double and maybe triple, her head pounding sickeningly, her movements too slow.

The blade came up again, and she slammed her fist into his throat, heard him gag as the knife clattered to the floor. She dove for it, landing with a thud, her fingers grasping the handle. She had it in her hand, and she was up, nearly blinded by the pain in her head, praying that the guy didn't have another weapon.

She expected him to come at her again, to try to wrest the knife from her grip, but he was gone, the corridor empty and quiet.

If she hadn't been holding the knife, she might have believed she'd imagined it all.

The doors he'd entered through were closed. None of the patients' rooms were open. There was a right turn at the end of the corridor, though. He must have run that way.

She wanted to go after him, but she was afraid to leave Beatrice. She was also afraid she wouldn't be quick or strong enough to apprehend him. She felt shaky and off balance, and that wasn't a good way to go into a battle.

She turned back to the room, fumbled with the doorknob, her grip clumsier than before, her heart beating hollowly in her ears. She needed to sit, but first she needed to buzz for a nurse, explain what had happened.

"Stella!" Chance called, and she turned, saw that he'd walked into the corridor and she hadn't even heard him.

His gaze dropped to the knife, jumped back to her face.

"What happened?" He took the knife from her hand, using his shirttail to keep from touching it. Then he cupped her cheek. His palm was warm and calloused, his touch light.

She wanted to lean into the comfort of it.

Lean into him, but she'd made her choice, and what

she'd chosen was to go it alone. Live life without the connections that could break a heart and bruise a soul.

"Some guy thought he could go through me and get to Beatrice," she said, and was surprised to hear the shakiness in her voice.

She never got shaky. Ever.

"That explains the fire in the stairwell," he muttered. "A great diversionary tactic. I shouldn't have left you here alone."

"How could you have known?" she asked.

"Easily. I shouldn't ever be surprised at the lengths a criminal will go to get what he wants. Did you get a good look at him?"

"He was wearing scrubs. I thought he was a nurse. He had dark brown hair. Tall. He was wearing a surgical mask, so I didn't see his face."

He didn't ask for more details. He already had his cell phone out, was dialing a number. Probably Cooper's. Or, maybe Boone's.

Seconds later, he tucked the phone away, set the knife on the ground and studied her face.

Carefully.

Thoroughly.

She wasn't sure what he was looking for.

Maybe signs of her weakness. Of her desperate need for support.

"Are you okay?" he finally asked.

"Yes."

"He didn't hurt you?"

"I didn't give him a chance."

He offered a grim smile.

"Typical," he said, and it didn't sound like a compliment.

"What's that supposed to mean?"

"Just that you could have called for help. There are nurses, doctors and security guards all over the place."

"I didn't have a whole lot of time to think about that. I barely had time to react," she said. No heat in her words. She was too tired for that. Too sick.

"Right. Sorry." He glanced at the knife. "He meant business."

"I know. I'm just glad I was able to keep him from getting to my grandmother."

"You're assuming he was going after her."

True.

She was.

Because of the rocks on the glass and the message Beatrice said she'd been given.

She would have told him that, but two security officers ran into the corridor, Boone right behind them. Everyone seemed to be talking at once, the noise tearing through Stella's skull.

She leaned against the wall, closing her eyes and trying to stop the whirling, swirling world.

Warm hands wrapped around her waist, slid along her sides, and she was being lifted, carried somewhere by someone. She'd have opened her eyes to see who, but she felt the edges of a silky tie brush her face, caught a whiff of pine needles and snow and familiar cologne.

"I can walk," she said without opening her eyes.

"And?" he responded, the words rumbling against her cheek.

"I *should* walk."

"We're not going far."

He set her down, and she finally opened her eyes.

He'd brought her back to Beatrice, and she was sitting in the chair by the bed again.

"Law enforcement will be here soon," Chance said, crouching in front of her. He had the bluest eyes she'd ever seen, the longest lashes, and if she hadn't been such a coward, she'd have stuck it out with him. Because he wasn't just handsome. He was smart, driven, kind. All the things any woman could want.

And she had wanted him.

She just hadn't wanted to lose him.

"I want you to rest until they get here. All right?" She could have argued.

She could have insisted that she should be out in the hall, helping him run the show. That's what she usually did, and he was usually happy enough to let her.

But she didn't think she could walk if she wanted to, and she didn't think she'd do anyone any good if she passed out in the hallway.

She nodded, wincing as pain shot through her head again.

"Good." He smiled, tucking a blanket around her, touching her cheek as if they were exactly what they should have been—a couple, tied together by years of seeing and meeting each other's needs.

She wanted to tell him how stupid she'd been, how foolish. She wanted to tell him how much she longed to go back to that day when she'd let him walk away and make a different choice, a braver one.

But her words seemed to be coming as sluggishly as her thoughts, and before she could even open her mouth, he was gone.

It was for the best.

She knew that.

So, why was she having such a difficult time believing it?

Chance didn't like being played for a fool. He liked it even less when someone he cared about was nearly killed because of it.

He closed the door to Beatrice's room and pulled out his phone, snapping a few pictures of the abandoned knife. He'd wanted to ask Stella if the guy had been wearing gloves, but she'd been so close to passing out, he'd decided to wait. Security was already combing the hospital, trying to find the perpetrator. A tall guy in scrubs with brown hair.

Only the guy had probably already changed back into street clothes and was moving through the hospital unchallenged by security guards. He'd be outside before law enforcement arrived with the K-9 team Chance had asked for.

"Strange-looking knife," Boone commented, crouching beside the weapon.

He was right. The blade looked typical enough, but there were odd symbols and pictures carved into the wooden handle. "Looks like an old bowie knife."

"*Old* being the operative word," Boone murmured. "Weird carvings, but the blade is all business."

"Yeah," Chance responded. "Stella said the guy was trying to get through her to get to Beatrice. I'm wondering why anyone would want to kill a lady who already has Alzheimer's."

"Inheritance? Does she have other family? Maybe someone who's a little too anxious to get that big old house and whatever money she might have?"

"Maybe. We'll check into it."

"But you think this is about Stella, right?" Boone straightened.

"It makes more sense."

"She's got more enemies, but that doesn't mean it makes more sense," Boone argued. "If someone wanted to go after Stella, why do it this way? Why not shoot her while she was walking outside? Set the house on fire? Plant a bo—"

"I'm sure I can think of just as many ways she could die as you can," Chance said dryly.

"All I'm saying is that Stella's grandmother is vulnerable. Without Stella to look out for her, she's an easy target for an accident like what happened tonight."

"You're saying someone wants Stella out of the way so he can get to Beatrice?" It was something Chance hadn't thought of.

"I'm not saying that's a fact. I'm just saying it's a possibility."

Maybe it was.

But accidents could happen with or without Stella dead. According to Stella, Beatrice still had an active social life, going to book club meetings with friends, participating in a women's mission group that met at church every week. She and Stella weren't always together.

"There are a lot of possibilities. I'm going to ask Trinity to do a little research for me, go back through the reports from some of Stella's more recent missions. Maybe there's a clue there. If she comes up empty, we'll know to focus things closer to home."

"Trinity never comes up empty," Boone said.

True. Chance's younger sister was an expert in computer forensics, was training to be a search and rescue worker, and had been an integral part of HEART for several years.

She excelled at finding people and at coordinating missions from headquarters. She kept track of the team members as they went out on missions, got them help quickly when they needed it. She also filed reports, wrote up bids and generally made things run a lot more smoothly than they would have without her.

Office work.

That's what Trinity called it.

Chance called it necessary and safe. His parents had

already lost one daughter, and he was going to make sure they didn't lose another. He'd been six years younger than his older sister. Old enough to remember her leaving for mission work. Old enough to remember his mother and father crying when they'd heard that the village she was working in had been attacked.

She'd been kidnapped, and she'd never been found.

He wasn't going to let that happen to Trinity.

He'd call her, ask her to do some research.

Maybe that would make her happier than she'd been in recent weeks.

"She never comes up empty, and she's never slow. That's going to pay off in this situation," he said, eyeing the knife. He'd already snapped a few pictures. He texted one to his sister. Asked her to find out what it was and if it was rare.

"You should have her look at Stella's personal life, too. Didn't she just break up with someone?"

"How should I know?" But he was pretty certain she hadn't been in a serious relationship with anyone since they'd broken up.

Boone snorted. "You know everything about everyone on the team. Especially Stella."

"What's that supposed to mean?"

"None of us are guaranteed another day. It would be a shame to wait for tomorrow only to find out that tomorrow isn't going to come."

"Since when did you become a philosopher?" he asked, and Boone grinned.

"Since always. It's one of my best characteristics."

"That and your ability to down more food than sixteen truckers?"

"Exactly. So didn't she just break up with someone?" Boone pressed for the answer that he knew Chance had, because he was right. Chance made it his business to know about his operatives' lives.

"If you're talking about the navy guy, they went out twice. I don't think saying no to a third date could be considered breaking up."

"He might be Navy. Stella mentioned him to my wife a few months ago."

"Like I said, they went out twice. I don't think that can be considered a breakup."

"Maybe you don't, but what about the guy she was with?"

Good question.

Stella didn't date often.

He knew that. Just like he knew that if she'd ever planned to be serious about anyone, it would have been him.

No pride in that thought.

Just honesty.

They were made for each other. Two halves of the same whole. As corny as it sounded, he thought it was true. If he'd been another kind of guy, he would have tried to prove it to her.

He wasn't, so he'd let her go.

And here they were—her dating life the subject of a conversation he'd rather not be having. He might keep close tabs on his team, but he tried hard not to stick his nose into their personal business.

"I'll have Trinity check into that relationship. Just to make sure the guy was in DC when all this went down."

He dialed his sister's number, waiting impatiently as the phone rang. He needed to find the guy who'd gone after Stella, and he needed to return to his life, because he could feel himself being pulled back into that nice little fantasy—the one where he and Stella were exactly what each other needed, where both of them were willing to admit it and where happily-ever-after became the ending they both longed for.

A pipe dream, and he'd never been much of a dreamer.

He was a doer, and what he was going to do was make certain Stella and her grandmother were safe. Then he was going back to DC, back to the life that only ever seemed lonely when Stella was around to remind him of what he was missing out on.

FIVE

Sheriff Cooper Brighton had been the town bad boy when Stella was growing up—the guy every girl wanted to be with, the boy every father distrusted and the rival every young man wanted to defeat.

Now he was the town sheriff, and he wore the uniform and the badge as easily as he'd worn the bad-boy label.

She watched him as he jotted something into his notepad, waiting impatiently for the next question. He'd asked at least a hundred already. Most of them just repeats of earlier ones. Same question worded in a different way.

At least he hadn't insisted that he conduct the interview somewhere besides Beatrice's room. He'd been agreeable and cooperative, telling Stella that they could talk wherever she felt most comfortable.

She felt most comfortable right beside Beatrice, Chance standing behind her. She didn't have to glance over her shoulder to assure herself that he was still there. She knew he was.

She also knew that Boone was outside the door, sitting in the chair again, firearm holstered beneath his jacket.

Beatrice was safe. For now.

"Is there anything you want to add to what you've told me?" Cooper finally asked, looking up from the pad and meeting her eyes.

There *was* something. It had been scratching at the back of her mind since the sheriff arrived, trying to catch and hold her attention. If she hadn't had the headache to end all headaches, she'd have already mentioned it.

"Beatrice said someone tossed rocks at her window and woke her up. She also said that he told her he had a message from Henry."

"Is that why she went outside this morning?" Cooper asked, and she nodded.

"That's what she said. It's possible she was confused."

"It's also possible that she wasn't," Chance broke in.

"I know. But I don't know why anyone would want to hurt her. What other motivation would someone have for luring her outside during a winter storm?"

"That's a good question." Cooper stood, grabbed his coat from the back of the chair and handed Stella his business card. "That's my direct number. I'm going back to your place. I want to see if there's any evidence that someone was outside Beatrice's window. Which room is she in?"

"It's at the back of the house. The far left window. Pink curtains."

"I bet Henry loved that," Cooper said, a half smile curving his lips. He'd always had a soft spot for her grandparents, because they'd never bought into the town's view of him. When he was a tween and teen, they'd given him odd jobs to do around the property, and they'd paid him well for the work.

"He loved anything that my grandmother loved."

"I know. And who could blame him? Beatrice has the best heart of anyone I've ever known. Remember that old donkey she insisted on rescuing? That thing was as ugly as sin. Swaybacked and old as the hills. She paid me to brush its tail and mane and put little pink ribbons in both." He glanced at Beatrice, smiling at the memory.

"I remember. Granddad was afraid she'd want you to paint its hooves pink, too."

"She asked. I refused. It was a male donkey. I figured it deserved a little dignity."

She laughed, the sound ending on a groan as pain shot through her already aching head.

"You okay?" Chance touched her shoulder, the warmth of his hand seeping through her damp flannel, chasing away some of the chill she hadn't realized she'd been feeling.

"I will be once we figure out what's going on."

"Hopefully that will be soon." Cooper shrugged into his coat. "Beatrice is a good lady. I'm going to do everything I can to make sure she stays safe. Call if you remember anything else. I've got a couple of guys going over the hospital security footage. I'll keep you updated." He walked out into the hall and disappeared from view.

"Here." Chance pressed a cup into her hand. "You need some sugar."

"I need some answers." She sipped the lukewarm orange juice, her stomach twisting. "I also need Tylenol."

"I have that, too." He handed her two tablets. "Cleared by the nurse, so it's safe to take."

"Did any of the nurses see the guy who attacked me?"

"They saw him. He had a badge, and they didn't bother checking his ID. The security guards already found it with the scrubs in a bathroom on the main floor."

"Near the lobby?" She swallowed the pills with the rest of the juice.

"Yes. The sheriff has a K-9 unit moving through. It's possible they'll track him."

"You know it isn't, Chance. He walked out the lobby door and he got in a car. He drove away in a vehicle that was either stolen or unregistered."

"Probably."

"There's no *probably* about it. We've done this thing dozens of times together. We know how it works."

"We know how it *usually* works. Let's leave some room for surprises, okay?" He pulled a chair up next to hers and took her hand, the gesture intimate and gentle, and so surprising she didn't pull away. They'd sat like this before. Years ago. When they'd thought they might be able to make something special out of the thing that was between them—the admiration, the respect, the chemistry that always seemed to steal Stella's breath.

She glanced away, her fingers curving through his, her heart slamming against her ribs.

"I've never liked surprises," she murmured, hoping he couldn't feel the wild throbbing of her pulse.

"Then leave room for possibilities. You seem to think the guy was coming after Beatrice. The team is checking into the theory that you're the target."

It was a possibility. She knew that. Her work put her in contact with lots of people who knew how to hold grudges and get revenge. Most of them were far away, and it would be difficult for them to get visas into the country. Money talked, though, and it could accomplish a lot.

"My last mission was in Egypt," she said as if he hadn't been there with her, as if they hadn't found a child kidnapped by her abusive father and brought her back to the United States. She'd known then just how wrong she'd been to close herself off to Chance. She'd had a dozen opportunities to tell him, a dozen moments when she'd wanted to.

Fear had kept her silent.

Fear of loving him and losing him.

Just like she had her family.

"We're checking the whereabouts of the people involved in that. Is there anyone else we should look into?"

"You know exactly what I've been involved in, where I've gone and who I've angered."

"I do, but we also need to think on a more personal level." He still had her hand, his thumb running across her knuckles. She could have been distracted by that if she let herself be, but she knew he was getting at something, moving toward a subject that he didn't think she'd want to discuss.

Her brain might be moving slowly, but she knew exactly what he was asking. She didn't care. Talking about her personal life—what little she had of it—didn't bother her. "There's no one in my life who'd want to kill me out of jealousy or anger. I don't have an ex-boyfriend stalking me, and I didn't rebuff some guy who might be holding a grudge."

"You've been out on a couple of dates recently."

"I didn't realize you were keeping track," she responded, a little hint of something zinging through her.

Happiness?

Pleasure?

It sure wasn't annoyance.

"The last date I went on was a week before my grandfather died. I haven't seen Noah since then."

"Maybe Noah isn't happy about that?"

"I'm sure he didn't give it a second thought. We're friends. That's all."

"Can I have his contact information? I'd like to verify that with him."

"No," she snapped, and then wished she hadn't. Beatrice stirred, moaning softly in her sleep. She looked tiny, the bed and linens nearly swallowing her up.

"Look," Stella continued more quietly. "Noah was a member of my husband's special ops unit. We've been friends for years. We went out because he'd broken up with his fiancée and was feeling lonely. That's it."

"If that's it, then why don't you want me to contact him?"

"The last thing Noah needs is people butting into his business." He'd been wounded during an operation three years ago, and he hadn't been the same since.

"It's not butting in to check on someone's whereabouts."

"Chance—"

"You can trust me to do things discreetly," he cut her off.

Any other day, she might have argued with him, given him a dozen reasons why she knew Noah hadn't been the guy who'd attacked her.

She stood instead, placing the juice on the table near Beatrice's bed and walking to the window. Snow still fell, drifting to the ground in huge flakes. She wanted to walk outside, let the frigid air clear the cobwebs from her head. More than that, she wanted to hunt down the guy who'd attacked her, make sure he didn't get another opportunity.

If she hadn't felt so weak, she might have left Chance with Beatrice and tracked down the K-9 unit that was searching for the perp, but she was weak, and she'd be stupid to go out looking for trouble.

"It's not a good idea to stand in front of the window, Stella," Chance cautioned, but he didn't pull her away and he didn't close the curtains.

He probably thought he was giving her what she wanted, what she always said she needed—space, distance, platonic friendship.

Except that they could never be friends, because they'd always been meant to be something more.

"I need to keep Beatrice safe," she murmured, trying to refocus her thoughts, keep them where they needed to be. "The guy who attacked me is still out there, and I can't count on him not returning."

* * *

Chance heard the worry in Stella's voice, and the weariness. She wasn't asking for help, but they both knew she needed it.

"We'll keep her safe."

We'll keep you *safe, too,* was on the tip of his tongue, but he didn't say it. Stella prided herself on being able to handle just about anything. She didn't like needing help, but she'd take it when necessary. This was one of the few times when it absolutely was.

"I appreciate that, Chance, but Cooper and his department—"

"Aren't going to be able to provide twenty-four-hour protection. HEART can."

"At what cost? Another job? A client who really needs your help not getting it because you're here helping me?"

"We have plenty of man power, Stella, and you know it. If you don't want us here, you'll have to come up with a better reason than that." She wouldn't. Because she knew HEART could do what needed to be done faster and better than just about anyone else.

He was as confident of that as he was that the sun would rise every morning.

She shrugged, her shoulders narrow and thin beneath her pajama top. He caught a glimpse of her scar again— purple against her pale skin. He knew a little about the story—that she'd been in a car accident that had killed her entire family. That she'd escaped with terrible burns.

And terrible nightmares.

She'd never told him that, but he'd heard her talking in her sleep more than once. They'd camped out in dozens of places with the team, and he'd heard her muttering about flames, and then saying a name over and over again.

Her sister's name.

When he let himself, he could imagine Stella as a little girl, trying desperately to save her sister from the fire.

"If you want HEART out, say so," he prodded, and she sighed.

"I would, but I do need the help. Much as I hate to admit it, my brain isn't functioning at a fast enough pace to keep Beatrice safe."

"It functioned fast enough to stop a knife attack."

"Muscle memory."

"And God?"

"He does always seem to come through for me. Even when I doubt that He will. I should probably learn something from that."

"Like?"

"I don't always have to fight my battles alone." She brushed hair from Beatrice's face, her palm settling on her forehead. "She feels warm."

"She's under a few blankets."

"Warm as in feverish." She pressed the call button for the nurse and removed one of the blankets that covered her grandmother. "I hope it's not pneumonia. She inhaled water, and she was hypothermic. She could—"

"Stop," he said, taking the blanket from her hand and setting it on the chair. They were so close he could see the flecks of violet in her blue eyes, see the gold tips of her red lashes. "Worrying won't change a thing."

"I'm not worrying. I'm speculating."

"That's not going to change anything, either."

"It's going to keep me going," she said, turning to her grandmother again, putting some space between them, because it would have been way too easy to walk into each other's arms.

Chance knew it, and he kept his distance, because there was more to a relationship than heat and passion. There was deep sharing and vulnerability and a dozen other things that Stella didn't want.

"Who says you have to keep going?" he asked, and she shrugged.

"Me. If I don't keep moving, I'm going to fall over. Then where will Beatrice be?"

"In this bed with me watching over her."

She looked like she was going to say something in response, but a nurse bustled in, her scrubs swishing as she moved to the bed.

"Is everything okay?" she asked, and Stella began filling her in, questioning whether or not X-rays had been ordered, asking if there'd been any sign of fluid in the lungs.

Chance could have waited for the answers, but he had other things to do, a few phone calls to make while Stella was focused on her grandmother.

He wanted to give Trinity Noah's name. She might be able to come up with a surname, maybe figure out who the guy was. HEART had plenty of contacts in the military, and it shouldn't take any time at all to track down a buddy of Stella's deceased husband. Daniel Silverstone was a military legend. Smart, quick and deadly, he'd died a hero's death, saving his unit from enemy fire. Stella never talked about him. She never talked about her marriage or what it had felt like to be widowed at such a young age. It was another reason why they'd broken up. Chance had wanted to know, and he hadn't understood her need to keep it from him.

"How are things going in there?" Boone asked as Chance stepped into the hall. He'd taken a seat in the chair again, his legs blocking half the corridor. To the untrained eye, he looked relaxed, but Chance sensed the tension in him. He was ready for more trouble.

They might get it, but it wasn't going to be at the hospital. Not with so many deputies and security guards roaming the hallways.

"Beatrice seems to be holding her own, but Stella's worried."

"I meant with the interview. Was she able to remember anything else?"

"Nothing that is going to help us put a name to her attacker. I do have the name of the last guy she dated."

"Noah Ridgewood?"

"She didn't give me a last name."

"It's Ridgewood. I texted Scout to see if she remembered."

"Thanks. I'm going to have Trinity see what she can dig up on the guy. I'm also going to have her call in another team member. You need to get home to your family."

"I can stay a few days. Scout will understand."

"Maybe, but your kids won't. They need you home when you can be there, and this isn't a paid mission. It's a favor for a friend."

Several HEART members had been married in the past year. Chance tried to give them as much family time as possible. It was important for their marriages, their homes and their work. If he had a wife and kids, they'd be his priority. God first. Then family. Then business.

That was the way his father had raised him.

It was the way he'd planned to be if he'd gotten married.

At this point, he doubted that would happen.

He'd found the woman he wanted to be with. He'd probably end up waiting a lifetime for her to realize she wanted to be with him.

He frowned, glancing at the door and calling himself every kind of fool for falling for Stella again and again and again.

"Kids do grow up fast at this age." Boone said. "And I have lots of lost time to make up for with Jubilee."

"You guys are doing okay, right?" Chance had asked the question so many times he was sure Boone was tired of it, but being reunited with a daughter who'd been missing for five years was challenging. Even in the best of circumstances.

"Better than I anticipated. She's a smart kid, and she's eager to fit in with the family. The counselor seems to think she's doing remarkably well."

"Anything I can do to help?"

"You've already done enough. You helped find her. You helped keep her safe. You gave me two months of leave." Boone shook his head. "I owe you. We both know it."

"A person can never owe family, Boone. We do what we can for one another, and we don't keep score."

"Exactly." Boone stood and stretched. "Keep that in mind when you're dealing with Silverstone."

"What's that supposed to mean?"

"She's been thrown off the horse more than once. It's not surprising she's afraid to get back on it."

"You're talking in riddles, and I'm not in the mood."

"I'll make it plain then. Family is everything. Stella is family. To me, she's like a sister. To you…" He shrugged. "You get to decide, but I'd say she's a lot more, and I'd say you'd be a fool to let her keep avoiding what you both so obviously want."

"And what, exactly, would that be?" he asked, irritated with the conversation and with the fact that Boone could read him and Stella so easily.

"Like I said, that's for you to decide. Just make sure you don't let the past get in the way of whatever the future could be. Family should never keep score of the good things, but we shouldn't keep score of the bad, either."

He pulled a bag out of his pocket. Not cookies this time. Chips. "You going to call your sister? Maybe we can get that information before the sun goes down."

"Sure," Chance said, gladly allowing the direction of the conversation to change. Whatever was between him and Stella, it was theirs to deal with. Hopefully, Boone would keep that in mind.

He dialed his sister's number as he walked to the end of the hall, following the same route the K-9 team had tracked earlier. Down a longer hall. Around another corner. Through doors that led into a stairwell.

The guy had run to the lobby, changed his clothes in a bathroom there and escaped completely unnoticed.

The security cameras had to have captured him, though. There were cameras in the stairwell and in the lobby. Chance was anxious to see the footage and to find out whether or not they'd gotten a clear picture of the guy's face.

Because if they had, he'd be that much closer to keeping Stella and her grandmother safe.

He left a message for Trinity as he walked into the hospital lobby. A few police officers were gathered there, a large German shepherd beside one of them. It looked like the K-9 team had followed the trail as far as it could and then returned to the hospital.

Chance wanted to know exactly where the trail had ended, what they had found at the end of it. A parking space? A dirt road? A shed or house of some sort?

There was no time like the present to find out.

He pasted on the easy smile he'd trained himself to use, the one that said he wasn't a threat, that he only wanted a friendly conversation. He'd learned long ago that he could catch more flies with honey than with vinegar, so he kept the vinegar for cleaning up messes and for making reluctant people give him the information he wanted.

The honey, though?

He used it as often as he needed it.

The officers eyed him as he approached, and he was sure they were noticing the bright tie and the starched white shirt, the tailored pants and jacket. He liked people to underestimate him, to assume he was a business man who just happened to run a hostage rescue team.

He introduced himself the same way he always did. Handshake, smile, business card. Once everyone was on the same page, he asked how the search had gone.

Next thing he knew, he was being given the tour, through the hospital lobby and out into the swirling snow. It was amazing that the dog had tracked anything in this, but it still seemed to have the scent. Nose down, it moved unerringly toward the corner of the building, around the side and then into a back lot that stretched into an empty field. They crossed that and moved onto a paved street in the town's main business section. Lots of buildings. Cars. Trucks. They passed a restaurant, a bank, a drug store, then went into the parking lot of a small movie theater.

"This is it," the K-9 officer said. "We have security footage from the theater's external camera. It shows the vehicle and the guy getting into it."

"You've already seen it?"

"Sure have." The officer was young, maybe midtwenties, and he seemed eager to prove himself. "Got the make of the car, but not the license plate, off it. No visual of the perp's face. If you want to take a look, I can check with the sheriff and see if he'll approve it."

"That would be great," Chance replied, eyeing the empty lot. He could see the tire tracks in the snow, nearly covered now but visible. The lot itself was behind the building and hidden from the street.

The perp must have known that.

Did that mean he knew the area? Or that he'd spent a few days staking it out, finding places where he could easily blend in and hide out?

Too many questions and not enough answers. Chance wanted to see that footage. Once he got a make and model for the vehicle, he could send the information to Trinity, see if she could connect it with any of Stella's known associates.

Or any of Beatrice's.

It was still possible that the attacker was after Stella's grandmother. Especially if Beatrice was right about rocks being thrown at the window. Boone had suggested inheritance as a motive, but Chance didn't know of any family aside from Stella who might benefit from the elderly woman's death.

He frowned, pulling out his cell phone as he followed the officer and dog back to the hospital. He texted Simon to ask him to check for evidence under the window. Sure, the sheriff was going to do that, but Simon knew how to assess a crime scene without disturbing it, and Chance needed to know exactly what had happened at the house. Then he texted Trinity and asked her to do some digging into Beatrice's family tree. Maybe someone, somewhere, would gain if Stella lost her grandmother.

He had to find out, and he had to do it quickly.

Whoever this guy was, he had motive, he had means, and he wasn't messing around. Two attempts in a few hours meant he was also desperate.

For what?

That was the question Chance needed to answer.

If he did, he'd have the answer to everything else.

Except what he was going to do once Stella was safe and there was nothing standing between them but her reluctance to be hurt and his decision to let her walk away.

SIX

They wheeled Beatrice out for a chest X-ray at midnight. Stella followed the nurse and orderly through the quiet hallway and into the elevator, her body heavy with fatigue, her mind numb with it. Chance stood a few feet away, grim and silent, his jaw shadowed with the faintest hint of a beard. He met her eyes but didn't speak. She knew he didn't approve of her leaving the room to follow Beatrice. He'd wanted her to stay behind the closed door, Boone guarding her until he returned.

Usually, she didn't care about other people's opinions. She did her thing, followed her gut. Generally with good results.

Right now, though, she wasn't thinking clearly, and that was a terrifying place to be.

Chance, on the other hand, was clearheaded. He'd told her that the best thing she could do was stay in the room. Then he'd let it drop.

Just like always.

That was the way Chance operated.

No fuss or muss. No debates. Just stating facts and expecting people to get on board with his logic because, most of the time, his logic was flawless.

Of course, this wasn't about logic.

This was about love, and Stella loved her grandmother too much to leave her alone and confused.

And she *was* confused.

She'd spent most of the day and night asking where she was, what had happened, where Henry was.

Even now, she was pulling at the oxygen mask, trying to drag it away so she could speak without her voice being muffled.

Stella reached for her hand, but Chance already had it. "Better leave that mask where it is, Ms. Beatrice," he said. "Your oxygen level is a little low."

"I'm sick?"

"Yes." He set her hand back on the gurney and patted it. "But you'll be better soon."

"You're Chance," Beatrice said as if she were trying to hold on to the name and remind herself of who he was. "Stella's friend."

"That's right."

"You two went out a few times."

"Nana," Stella cut in hurriedly. "Chance and I work together."

"I know that, dear, but you *did* date."

"Now you choose to remember things?" she muttered, and Chance laughed, steering her out of the elevator as the doors opened. They went toward radiology and Stella would have walked in, but the nurse shook her head.

"Sorry. Only patients past this point. We'll bring her out to you when she's done. It shouldn't be long."

They rolled her away, and Stella wasn't sure what to do with herself. She'd spent most of the day sitting in the seat beside Beatrice or pacing the ICU trying to piece together how they'd gotten there. She'd run everything through in her mind dozens of times, and she still didn't have any answers that made sense.

Things had been fine since her grandfather's funeral.

She hadn't sensed any trouble. Aside from Beatrice's health, there'd been nothing to worry about. Just everyday things to take care of. Even that hadn't been difficult. Her great-uncle Larry was a financial planner, and he knew exactly what Beatrice had, what Henry had left her and how long she could support herself without digging into retirement funds.

A long time.

Probably much longer than she'd live.

That had surprised Stella. Henry had been a pastor, and he hadn't made much money. She'd learned to live frugally when her grandparents were raising her. The house was beautiful. The antiques it contained stunning. But they were Beatrice's heritage, an inheritance from a father and grandfather who'd left her much wealthier than Stella would have ever guessed.

Stella's childhood had been nice, but modest. She'd had what she needed. Nothing more. No big parties or expensive clothes. Nothing excessive. She'd worked for her own car, and she'd paid for the gas and insurance on it. She hadn't minded. She'd been too grateful to her grandparents to ever complain that she didn't have the fanciest or most expensive things.

"Worried?" Chance asked, his hand settling between her shoulder blades.

"About Beatrice? Yes."

"About everything," he responded.

She turned to face him and realized just how close they were. Barely a breath between them, his bright tie at eye level, hanging loose. She tugged at the end of it, pulling it from his neck and tucking it into his shirt pocket.

"It's a little late in the day for a tie, don't you think?" she asked, avoiding his comment because she really didn't want to go into all the reasons why she was worried.

"It's a little late in the day for avoiding my questions, don't you think?"

"Probably," she admitted, turning away, not wanting to look into his beautiful eyes. She knew what she'd see there. The same compassion and understanding she saw when he was questioning clients or reassuring a victim. He had a way of making people open up to him.

She didn't like opening up to anyone.

She didn't like feeling vulnerable.

She *hated* being on the receiving end of pity.

She'd felt all of those things in the past few hours, and she needed some time to regroup, get herself together, take a little control back.

"Not talking about it isn't going to make it go away," Chance pointed out as she dropped into one of the chairs.

"Talking about it won't help, either."

"Stop lobbing volleys, Stell. If we're going to find the guy who attacked you, we need to work together."

"We are working together. I told you everything I know."

"Not Noah's contact information."

"Are we back to that?" She sighed, pulled her knees up to her chest and rested her chin on them.

"You need to trust me to handle things the way they need to be handled." He sidestepped the question, got right back to his point.

"Unless I've missed my guess," she muttered, turning her head just enough to meet his dark blue eyes, "you've already obtained Noah's full name, his address, his last known whereabouts. So why bring this up again?"

"You're not the only one who's worried. I don't want to see anything happen to you or your grandmother, and I can't do my job effectively with one hand tied behind my back."

"I'm not tying anything. I'm setting boundaries."

"Boundaries that are going to get you killed." His words were calm, his voice quiet, but the irritation in his eyes was impossible to miss.

"You're angry about nothing, Chance. If I'd thought that Noah—"

"You have a concussion. Do you actually believe you're making a rational assessment of the situation?" He stood, pacing across the room, his hands shoved into the pockets of his suit jacket.

"Probably not," she admitted. "But I know Noah well. We've been friends for years. There's no way—"

"There's always a way, Stella," he said gently, and she had a cold, horrible feeling that he knew something she didn't.

"What did you find out about Noah?"

"His ex-fiancée filed for a restraining order two days ago. She said he's been abusive and violent for the past year."

"I don't believe her. Noah is about the least violent person I know."

"She had proof enough to convince a judge that she needed the order of protection." He stalked back toward her, his legs long and muscular beneath his black dress pants. Most days he looked like an easygoing businessman, but Stella had seen him fight. She'd seen him win against powerful opponents. She knew just how dangerous he could be, and just how smart.

If he was worried about Noah, she should be worried, too.

But…Noah?

They'd been friends for a decade. She'd seen him at his best and at his worst, and she'd never ever seen him lay a hand on anyone.

"I'll talk to him. See what the order of protection is all about." She didn't have her phone with her, but there was one in Beatrice's room.

"He hasn't been at his apartment in a week. And my guess is he won't be answering his cell."

"How do you know?"

"Trinity talked to a few neighbors, called his work. Noah took a ten-day vacation. It started a week ago."

"And?"

"I'm interested to see if he returns home in three days and goes back to work."

"He will," she insisted, but she wasn't really sure. "He's just looking for a change. He told me that. He's tired of climbing the corporate ladder. He's been talking about rejoining the DC police department."

"That will be difficult to do with a restraining order out against him. A restraining order he apparently felt no need to mention to you. Why do you think that is?" he asked, his expression cold and hard.

"I'm not sure, but I'm guessing you're going to give me some ideas."

"Maybe the change he really wanted is you in his life, Stella. Maybe he was looking for a little more than what you were willing to give. Maybe he didn't tell you about the restraining order because he didn't want to scare you off, and when you stopped seeing him, maybe he got a little angry. Maybe he wanted a little revenge."

"That's a lot of maybes, and a lot of speculation about a guy who isn't around to defend himself."

She did not want to believe that Noah had anything to do with the attack.

She *didn't* believe it.

Footsteps sounded in the hall, voices drifting into the waiting area. She thought the nurse and orderly had returned with Beatrice, but Simon strode into the room, his black hair falling across his forehead, his light-colored eyes cutting from her to Chance and back again.

"Law enforcement is finished at the house. I locked up." He handed Stella her purse. "The keys are in there. I tossed your phone in, too, but I don't know if it's charged."

"Thanks."

"How's your grandma?" he asked, a hint of a Southern drawl in his voice.

"We're waiting on X-rays. Was someone out in the hall with you?" She was sure she'd heard voices.

"Yeah." His gaze shifted to Chance. "Don't blow a gasket over this, Miller."

"Over wh…?"

Chance's words trailed off as a pretty young woman walked into the room. Tall, slender, honey-blond hair, freckles. The same dark blue eyes as her brother.

Trinity Miller.

There was absolutely no doubt in Stella's mind that Chance really was going to blow up about it because he'd hired Trinity to work at headquarters. He'd never had any intention of letting her work in the field. He'd told Trinity that. He'd told Stella that. He'd told everyone at HEART that. He'd lost one sister, and he had no intention of losing another.

Stella understood that.

She supported it.

Trinity was young. She was a little naive. She'd spent most of her life being protected and cared for by her very well-meaning family. She had no business walking into the kind of situations HEART went into every day.

Stella had talked to Trinity about it, explaining everything in detail, telling her just how dangerous this line of work was and just how easily she could break her family's heart by being hurt or killed.

Stella had thought Trinity understood, but here she was. In the flesh. And unless Stella was mistaken, she had a gun holster strapped on beneath her coat.

Chance had taught his sister to use firearms.

He'd taught her self-defense.

He'd taught her everything she needed to know to survive, but there was no way in the world he was going to let her walk into this situation.

He didn't know why she'd come.

He didn't know what she thought she was going to add to the investigation beyond the information she'd already dug up for them.

What he did know was that she wasn't going to stay.

Not if he had anything to do with it.

"Go home," he said.

Trinity had the nerve to sashay across the room, kiss his cheek and smile.

"It's good to see you, too, bro."

"Bro?"

"Would you rather me call you 'Killjoy'?"

"I'd rather you were back at headquarters," he retorted, not bothering to keep the edge out of his voice. He had enough to worry about. He didn't want to add his sister to the list.

"You said you needed someone to take Boone's place. Here I am." She opened her arms wide, and he could see her shoulder holster under her thick pink parka.

"You are not taking Boone's place," he said, and she frowned.

"I don't see why not."

"Did you tell Jackson you were coming?" He sidestepped her comment, knowing that she hadn't consulted with their brother. Jackson was the co-founder of HEART, and he was just as protective of Trinity as Chance was.

"I left a note at the office."

"Coward," he muttered, and her smile broadened.

"No. Just smart. I figured by the time he read it, it would be too late for him to sabotage my car or come up with some busy work for me to do."

"That would have been fine by me. In case you haven't gotten the hint, I don't want you here."

"Because you don't think I can handle it. But I can." She brushed past him and wrapped her arms around Stella.

"I'm so glad you're all right," she said, and Chance knew she meant it from the bottom of her heart. He still wasn't going to let her take Boone's place. He'd call Jackson and have him send someone else, but it wouldn't hurt for Trinity to stick around. She'd be good for Stella, and she'd be good for Beatrice. She had that kind of personality—the kind that made people comfortable. He appreciated that about her, but she loved her family and friends with the kind of zealous loyalty that could get her into all kinds of trouble if she let it.

"Thanks, sweetie," Stella said, extracting herself from the hug and smiling at Trinity. "But your brother is probably right. You should go home."

"Give me a break, Stella. You've seen me on the gun range, and you've seen me in training. You know I can handle this. Besides, I have some information that I thought you might be interested in."

"About Noah?" Stella's smile fell away, and she took Trinity's arm, dragging her to the seats and pulling her down into one.

"Actually, no. The last record I have of him is a plane ticket he bought two weeks ago. Baltimore–Washington International to Dallas–Fort Worth."

"Fort Worth? I wonder who he knows there," Stella murmured.

Trinity shrugged. "I have no idea, but I can tell you this. Your uncle has a lot to gain if something happens to your grandmother."

"I don't have an uncle," Stella replied.

"Great-uncle. Your grandmother's brother."

"Uncle Larry?" Stella asked.

Trinity nodded as she pulled a folder out of her oversize bag, thumbed through some papers and pulled one out. "See this?"

She thrust the paper toward Stella and jabbed at the top of it. "This is your great-grandfather's last will and testament. When he passed, his wife was already dead. He bequeathed his estate to your grandmother and great-uncle, and he had an executor make sure it was divided equally."

"And?" Stella took the paper from Trinity, her brow furrowed as she scanned the document. "As far as I know there was never any conflict between my great-uncle Larry and Beatrice regarding the estate."

"I couldn't find anything to disprove that theory. No legal action. No lawyers. Everything seems to have gone off without a hitch. The thing is, I searched online databases and found the name of your grandfather's attorney."

"William Tate. I could have saved you some effort and given the information to you, if you'd asked."

"I was just working off a hunch, and I didn't want to bother you." Maybe not, but Trinity must have thought she should have. Her cheeks were bright pink, her gaze lowered as she pulled another sheet from the folder. "Mr. Tate wouldn't tell me much, but he did say your grandfather was his client. Did you know that your grandmother is not?"

"The subject never came up," Stella said wryly.

"Do you know if your grandmother has a will?"

"Another subject that never came up."

"It needs to." Trinity held out the second sheet. "See

this? It's an addendum to your great-grandfather's will. Written about three months before he died. He left the house to your grandmother along with all its contents. She has the legal right to bequeath it to whomever she wants, but if she dies without a will, the house goes to your great-uncle."

Stella took the paper and read it, her brow furrowed. She looked intrigued and a little anxious, as if she was worried that there might be something to Trinity's find.

Chance was intrigued, too.

He'd have asked to see the paper, but Stella passed it to him, handing it over before he could.

"I'll admit that it looks bad," she said as he scanned it. "But there is no way my great-uncle would try to kill Beatrice to get the house. He and my great-aunt love Beatrice and were close to my grandfather."

"Love of money is the root of all evil," Trinity said. "And it can motivate people to do some really horrible things. I ran a credit check on Larry, and he's having some serious trouble paying his bills. He's three months behind on his car. The boat? He's behind on that, too. I called a couple of his buddies at the country club and—"

"Enough." Chance cut her off before she could go any further. He loved his sister, but she wasn't thinking about Stella's feelings. She was thinking about proving herself.

"There's plenty more," she said, her cheeks pink. She obviously knew she'd gone too far, and she glanced at Stella. "I'm sorry, Stell. I should have given you the write-up instead of shouting it to the world."

"It's okay. I know you're just trying to help," Stella said, her face ashen. "Larry is out of town. I don't think he's involved in any of this, but I'll talk to him. See what he has to say."

Trinity frowned. "You know your uncle better than

any of us. If you don't think he's involved, you're probably right."

"I think I'm right. I hope I am, but it still bears checking out. I called Larry earlier to let him know that Beatrice was in the hospital. Hopefully, I'll hear from him soon." She stood stiffly, her cheeks gaunt. She hadn't eaten and the last thing Chance had seen her drink was the few sips of orange juice.

"Tell you what," he said, cupping Stella's elbow and leading her back into the corridor. "How about we go back to the house once your grandmother is finished? You can shower, put on some warmer clothes, get something to eat."

"Food," she muttered, "would not be my friend right now."

"Juice, then," he insisted, and she sighed.

"Chance, I can take care of myself. I've always been able to take care of myself."

"That's the problem, isn't it, Stella? You can always take care of yourself, and you're never willing to let anyone step in and help out even when you really need it. You don't want to be vulnerable, but right now, you are. How about you just admit it, and we move on?" The words slipped out, and she frowned.

"You want me to admit it? Fine. I'm vulnerable right now, and you've helped me plenty. We both know it, and I appreciate it, but I can't leave Beatrice. She'll—"

"Be fine, Stella. Boone and Simon know what they're doing, and they're not going to let anything happen to her."

"Your sister knows what she's doing, too. She dug up a lot of information very quickly."

"My sister has a big mouth and doesn't know when to keep it shut."

"I heard that," Trinity called as she stepped into the

hall. "Sadly, I can't argue with it. I really am sorry, Stella. I was so excited to have something to share—"

"You don't need to apologize."

"I do, and I have. Twice, because I feel terrible. And now I'm going to agree with my brother for probably the first time ever. You need to go home for a while. You look like death warmed over."

"You were eavesdropping," Stella accused.

"I was, and it didn't make me agree any less."

"I'll make a note of that," Stella murmured, her gaze on the radiology department doors. Maybe she thought if she stared long enough, they'd open.

"Notes don't do squat if we don't learn from them," Trinity responded, and for the first time in a long time, Chance wanted her to just keep on doing what she was doing, because he needed the break, too.

He needed a few minutes away from the hospital and the bright lights and the people. He needed to look into Stella's eyes, make sure that she really was okay before he decided whether or not to let her stay involved in the investigation.

Sure, it was her problem and her trouble, but she was emotionally invested. That could be dangerous for all of them. If he thought she couldn't handle it, if he thought she was going to get herself or someone else hurt, he'd put her under armed protection until the team figured things out. She wouldn't like it, but she'd allow it.

He knew she would. For her grandmother's sake.

Stella was pragmatic. She understood how easily emotion could sway judgment.

She was also hard-core and determined, willing to do anything to achieve a goal.

That came with a price.

It wore a person down, made him want to hide away

for a while, sit in solitude and replenish the stores that had been depleted.

He frowned.

Yeah. He knew that feeling. He'd been there a lot lately.

Maybe Stella knew it, because she touched his wrist, cool fingers against his warm skin.

Nothing else.

No words.

No arguments.

No concern that Trinity was a few steps away, watching them both.

He didn't care, either.

Everyone on the team knew that he and Stella had dated. Everyone on the team thought they belonged together.

In his opinion, everyone on the team was right.

All he had to do was convince Stella of that.

He captured her hand when she would have pulled away, linking their fingers and pressing a kiss to her knuckles. She seemed surprised, but she didn't pull away.

"What was that for?" she asked.

"It's a promise," he responded, "that everything is going to be okay."

And then the double doors swung open and Beatrice was wheeled out.

SEVEN

Stella waited in Beatrice's room until the X-ray results were in and her grandmother was sound asleep, her raspy breath filling the room. Pneumonia. That was the verdict the doctor had given. He'd put Beatrice on an antibiotic and upped her oxygen. In a few days, he hoped to wean her off that and get her out of the ICU.

A few days.

That seemed like a lifetime to Stella. She wanted to bring Beatrice home now, back to the familiarity of her bed and her bedroom, fix her favorite tea and feed her one of the fancy chocolates she loved so much.

Since she couldn't do that, she'd go home, get her grandmother's robe and her spare slippers, maybe even one of the pretty nightgowns Beatrice loved so much. Then she'd grab the brush Beatrice kept on her nightstand, the loose powder that she liked to pat on her cheeks, the well-worn Bible that sat on the rocking chair. Beatrice might not be able to use any of those things, but it would make her feel better to have them nearby.

That was all Stella cared about.

That and figuring out what was going on and how to stop it.

And then there was Chance. The kiss on her knuckles

that she could still feel. Those whispered words—*It's a promise that everything is going to be okay.*

She'd been trying to put both out of her mind, but of course, she couldn't. Because she could never put Chance out of her mind. He was always there. The one guy who could be everything to her if she let him.

She grabbed her purse and tossed her phone into it. The battery was dead, and it was useless. She'd grab the charger when she went home.

"You going somewhere?" Trinity asked, looking up from the book she'd been reading. She'd taken position near the window, the oversize chair she was sitting in squeaking every time she moved. She looked tired and she looked young.

Stella could understand why Chance wanted her to return home.

She could also understand why Trinity had refused.

She'd been begging to take a more active part in HEART rescues, but neither of her brothers would allow it. She probably thought this was the perfect opportunity to prove her mettle. No need to get a visa, no need for pre-planning or travel approval. Just hop in a car and drive to a small town, bring information that might prove valuable, take part in the investigation on the ground rather than in the corner office at HEART headquarters.

If Stella had been in Trinity's shoes, she'd probably have done the same.

"I'm going back to the house. I want to get a few things for my grandmother."

Trinity set the book down and stood. "Does my brother know?"

"He will." He and Boone had gone to look at security footage obtained by the sheriff's department. If she hadn't been worried sick about Beatrice, Stella would have insisted on going with them.

"You know you can't go by yourself, right?"

"Seeing as I don't have a ride, yes."

"Even if you had a ride, it wouldn't be smart."

"I know, Trinity."

"So what are you going to do if Chance is still at the sheriff's office?"

"Find another ride."

"That's not a good idea."

"It wasn't a good idea for you to come here, but you did it anyway."

"I'm not the one who was nearly killed." She returned to the chair, picked up the book. "But you're an adult. You can make your own decisions."

"And you're going to text Chance as soon as I walk out the door."

"Something like that." Trinity smiled. "As a matter of fact, I may as well do it now." She pulled the phone from her pocket. "Or you can call and see if he's finished yet."

"Good idea." She took the phone, dialed Chance's number.

He picked up immediately.

"Trinity, we're not discussing anything unless it's you going home," he growled.

"It's Stella, and home is exactly where I was planning to go. That's why I'm calling. Are you still with Cooper?"

The door opened, and Chance walked in, tucking his phone away. "We just got back."

"And?" she asked, relieved that Chance was there and surprised by the feeling. She'd never needed Daniel. Not ever. Not when they'd met. Not when they'd married. Not when she'd spent long nights alone. She'd been happy when he'd returned, but she'd never been relieved, never felt the weight of responsibility, the burden of it, lifting as he walked through the door.

She'd felt that when Chance walked in. Felt it even more when he crossed the room and stood beside her.

"The perp must have known exactly where the cameras were. He kept his face hidden. No prints on the knife. No ID on the vehicle."

"That's not what I was hoping for."

"Me, neither." His gaze cut to Trinity who was studiously looking at her book. "We both know you're listening to every word. How about you don't pretend otherwise?"

"I was trying to avoid your wrath." She set the book on the window ledge and stood, taking her phone from Stella's hand. "But if you want to go head-to-head in front of Stella, that's fine."

"There's no need. I've already called Jackson. We agree that you should stay."

"Really?" She looked surprised and doubtful.

"As long as you follow instructions and do your part, yes."

"What, exactly, is my part going to be?"

"Sit with Beatrice when Stella can't be here."

"Fine," she agreed.

"That was a little too easy," Chance muttered.

"You give me what I want, I make your life easy. This is a good lesson for both of us," Trinity said solemnly. "Now you two go on and have fun. I'll take care of things here."

"Are you sure—" Stella began, because she was worried about her grandmother, terrified that she'd wake up and be confused and scared.

"I won't leave her side," Trinity promised.

"Okay." Stella touched her grandmother's cheek, remembering all the times Beatrice had done the same for her. Remembering those long, painful days and nights after the accident when the only thing that had kept her from giving up was her grandmother's soft hand against her cheek, her quiet words, her fervent prayers.

"God be with you," she whispered in her grandmother's ear, remembering the words she'd heard so many times, "when I cannot. God give you strength when mine is not enough for both of us. God give you hope when we both feel hopeless, and when I am gone, may He give you love that stretches beyond this world and into the next."

She kissed Beatrice's temple, told herself she wasn't going to cry.

"That was beautiful," Trinity said quietly.

Chance didn't say a thing. Just took her arm and led her out of the room, down the hall, into the elevator. And she was still trying not to cry. Still telling herself that she had nothing to cry about.

The first tear fell as they stepped outside.

The second one fell as she slid into the passenger seat of Chance's SUV.

He still didn't say a word. Just rounded the side of the vehicle and got in, turning on the engine and the heat.

She sniffed back more tears. Annoyed. Irritated.

Broken.

Because she was more tired than she'd ever been before. Because her head hurt and her stomach churned and the one man who could always make her feel better was sitting right beside her, and she wouldn't reach for him because she was too much of a chicken.

"I don't cry," she felt the need to say.

"Everyone cries sometimes, Stella. Even me."

"I've never seen it."

"You've never seen me stand at the hospital bed of someone I love, either." He leaned toward her, his lips brushing her temple, her cheek, her lips.

She should have told him to stop, but she wanted more. Of him. Of this.

When he backed away, she wanted to follow, wanted to cling to his solid strength.

"Are you going to ask me what that was for?" he asked, his voice raspy and rough.

"Are you going to tell me?"

"It's a promise, Stella, that I'm not walking away from you. Not again."

He pulled out of the parking lot, the silence thick and filled with a dozen protests she could have made.

Didn't make, because she didn't want him to walk away.

Finally, he broke the silence. "I asked the sheriff about your uncle."

"And?"

"He said that Larry is a good guy who seems to really love his family. Including his sister and you."

"I agree."

"Sometimes people aren't what they seem."

"I agree with that, too."

"Did Larry return your call?"

"Not yet."

"Do you think that's odd?"

"He might have his phone turned off. People do that at night."

"Some people do, but would he?"

"I don't know."

"Do you want me to have some people track him down?"

"If he doesn't call tomorrow, we're not going to have a choice."

"Do you have any idea where he was going?"

"His property in Florida. He heard the storm was coming in, and he and Aunt Patty wanted to avoid it."

"When did he make the plans?"

"The first I heard of it was a week ago. Aunt Patty

mentioned it when she came to visit. She was excited. Usually, they don't go until after Christmas."

"That's what she said?"

"Yes."

"And a sudden winter storm changed all that, huh?" He turned into the snow-covered driveway, headlights splashing across tracks left from dozens of other vehicles.

The house jutted up from the landscape, black against the grayish sky, a light on in the attic and one on in the living room. A car was parked close to the porch, the paint gleaming dully in the moonlight. She thought it was familiar, but she couldn't quite place it.

"I wonder whose—" The attic light went off, and the rest of the sentence caught in her throat.

Chance thrust his phone into her hand. "Call the sheriff." He put the vehicle into Park. "And stay put."

Then he was out of the SUV, sprinting toward the house.

Whoever had entered the house was going to exit it.

Chance had no doubt about that.

Front door or back?

That was the question.

He sprinted up the porch stairs, tried the knob and wasn't surprised when the door swung open. He stepped inside, listening for the sound of footsteps. The house seemed empty, the silence echoing hollowly as he moved deeper into the foyer.

He glanced in the living room, the bright light there revealing a room that had been torn apart. Books pulled from shelves. Couch cushions tossed on the floor. A lamp had been overturned, the bulb shattered.

He flicked off the light, backing out of the room and leaving it for the police to process.

Right now, he had more important things to deal with.

There were servant stairs that led from the upper levels into the kitchen. If Chance were the one trying to avoid detection, he'd take those and go out the back door. He moved through the hallway, tensing as someone walked into the house behind him.

Stella. He could hear her pant cuffs brushing against the floor, hear the whisper of her breath as she stepped closer.

She didn't ask questions, didn't offer a plan, just kept pace with him as he walked into the kitchen. Like the foyer and hallway, it was empty, a small light above the stove illuminating the darkness. He flicked it off and walked to the servant stairs. The stairwell was pitch-black, the silence eerie.

Someone was there.

He could feel it like he felt the flash of adrenaline that shot through his blood.

He pulled out his Glock, motioning for Stella to move back. Somewhere above, a floorboard creaked. Then another. The perp was retreating, probably heading back toward the front steps.

Chance followed, the sound of creaking boards and running feet carrying through the house.

He reached the front stairs, saw a shadowy figure barreling down them. He didn't announce his presence, didn't give the guy a chance to see him. He lunged, forearm to throat, gun pressed to the underside of the jaw, slamming the guy up against the wall.

"Don't move," he growled, knowing the barrel of the gun was digging into flesh and his forearm was cutting off air. "Understand?" he asked, and the guy didn't nod. He whimpered.

"Do you have him?" Stella called.

"Yeah. Get the lights," he responded.

Seconds later, the foyer lit up, and he was looking into

the face of a man who had to be in his seventies. Salt-and-pepper hair, tan skin, blue eyes.

Larry Bentley.

Stella's great-uncle.

Chance had met the guy at Henry's funeral.

He eased his hold and backed off.

"You have any weapons on you, Larry?" he asked, and the older man shook his head, his hand trembling as he smoothed his hair.

"Of course not! I'm not a hoodlum." Larry's gaze darted to Chance's gun and then settled on his face again. "What's the meaning of this? Why are you in my sister's house?" he demanded.

"I was going to ask you the same thing."

"Uncle Larry?" Stella walked into the foyer, her skin nearly translucent with fatigue. "What are you doing here?"

"Picking up a few things for Beatrice. I planned to head to the hospital when I was done."

"At two in the morning?" she asked.

"She's my sister. She's ill. Does it really matter what time it is?"

"What I'd like to know," Chance said, "is why you were in the attic."

"I told you," Larry huffed. "I was looking for some things to bring to Beatrice."

"Is that why you tore the living room apart?"

"What?" Stella brushed past and stalked into the living room. She muttered something under her breath, and then returned, her eyes flashing with anger.

"What were you thinking?" she demanded, and Larry frowned.

"I didn't make that mess. It was already like that when I got here. I thought maybe the police had gone through the room looking for evidence."

"How did you even know that the police were here?" she asked. "I didn't tell you that in the message I left."

"Cooper left a message, too. He said they were conducting a full investigation."

"And to do that they needed to tear apart Nana's house? Come on, Uncle Larry," she said. "You're smarter than that."

"No need to get riled up, Stella. Like you said, it's the wee hours of the morning, and my brain isn't functioning well. I traveled all day to get here, and I drove straight from the airport to the house."

"You could have let me know you were on the way," Stella responded. She didn't look mollified by his explanation.

Chance wasn't, either.

"I would have, but I left my cell phone in Florida. I was in such a hurry after I heard the news, I guess I wasn't thinking straight."

Either that, or he hadn't wanted anyone to be able to track his movements. "What time did you arrive at the house?" Chance asked.

"Twenty minutes ago." He glanced at his watch. "Maybe a little longer."

"It took you a long time to gather things for your sister."

"I was looking for something specific. A wedding photo of our parents. It was in a beautiful Victorian frame. My great-grandmother's wedding brooch was worked into the frame. Do you remember it, Stella?"

"Of course. I saw it every day when I was growing up."

"It was on the fireplace mantel right before Henry passed," Larry said. "I haven't seen it since. I thought maybe Beatrice put it in her room or stored it in the attic."

"Why would she do that?" Stella walked into the living room, and Chance followed, watching as she studied the fireplace mantel. There were a few items there. A blue vase. A photo of Stella when she was ten, her bright red hair hanging nearly to her waist. Another one of Beatrice, Henry and Stella, all of them standing in front of the house, smiling at the camera. Stella was even younger in this one, the scars on her shoulder and upper arm revealed by a yellow tank top.

"Why does she do anything lately?" Larry responded.

"We could talk about that forever," Stella said, her gaze on the bookshelf and the books that had been pulled from it. "I'd rather talk about what happened here. If you didn't make this mess—"

"I didn't."

"Someone else did, then. Not the police. Cooper would never allow his deputies to leave a mess like this."

"Did you check any of the other rooms?" Chance asked, because if someone had been searching the house, it seemed unlikely he would have only torn apart the living room.

"I came in here and I went to the attic. That was it."

And yet, he'd been there twenty minutes.

Seemed like a long time to spend in two rooms.

Chance met Stella's eyes, saw his doubt reflected in her gaze.

Outside, emergency lights flashed as the sheriff's squad car raced up the driveway.

"Here comes the cavalry," Chance said. "Let's see what they have to say."

"I need to get those things for my grandmother," she responded, turning and heading up the stairs.

He wanted to follow, but Larry was hovering on the living room threshold, and Chance had the strange feeling that he was waiting for an opportunity to leave the scene.

Wasn't going to happen.

The guy had some explaining to do, and Chance was going to make sure he did it.

He offered a smile that he knew was anything but

friendly, tucked his Glock into its holster and opened the front door. He waited there as the sheriff got out of his vehicle and headed across the snowy yard.

EIGHT

Four days after she'd been knocked unconscious, Stella was finally beginning to feel more like herself. A mild headache, an ugly bruise and itchy stitches were a small price to pay for surviving what could have been deadly.

She couldn't complain.

Especially with Beatrice improving so much.

After two nights, her condition had been upgraded, and she'd been moved out of the intensive care unit. The private room she'd switched to had plenty of room for a cot, and the nursing staff had been happy to provide one for Stella. That had made it easy to keep an eye on Beatrice *and* rest.

She'd have rested better if Trinity hadn't insisted on bringing a tiny Christmas tree into the room. The potted plant stood about a foot high, its spindly branches barely covered by needles. Trinity had tried to make up for that by wrapping it in gold tinsel and decorating it with miniature ornaments.

For the past two nights, Stella had lain on the cot, staring at that tree, willing herself not to have nightmares. She'd thought of a dozen different ways she could get rid of the thing. Sneak it out in the middle of the night, toss it into the Dumpster behind the hospital, give it to the lady across the hall who never seemed to have any visitors.

Beatrice, of course, loved the tree.

As a matter of fact, she hadn't stopped talking about it.

"It's such a lovely little tree, don't you think, dear?" she asked for the umpteenth time, and, for the umpteenth time, Stella smiled and agreed.

"It is."

"We could hang stockings, too. Wouldn't that be nice?"

"I can—" Trinity began, and Stella shook her head. Sharply.

"We'll do that when you go home. We can get the stockings out of the attic and hang them from the fireplace mantel. Like we used to."

"Let's go, then." Beatrice sat up, the frilly nightgown she'd insisted on changing into hanging from her bony shoulders. She was still attached to an IV, and Stella put a hand on her arm, holding her in place.

"We will. Once the doctor releases you."

"When will that be?"

"Tomorrow. If you're still feeling good."

"Will that be a Sunday? I feel like I missed church this week. Did I?"

"Tomorrow is Tuesday. Yesterday was Sunday. Your friends came to visit you after church, remember?" Beatrice had had a steady stream of visitors since she'd left the ICU.

Chance had kept a list of every one of them.

He'd also made a list of people who'd visited Beatrice in the weeks after the funeral, because the framed photo hadn't been found. Someone had removed it. Larry had insisted it wasn't him, and Stella wanted to believe him.

Except for the fact that he really was in financial trouble, and the brooch that had been built into the frame was twenty-four-carat gold with a two-carat diamond surrounded by sapphires. Early twentieth-century Tiffany.

Stella had always thought the piece was paste.

She'd been wrong.

If she'd known it was worth nearly ten thousand dollars, she'd have asked her grandparents to lock it in the safe long ago.

Larry and Patty had traveled to Florida. They could have brought the piece with them, sold it to some antiques dealer somewhere and pocketed the money.

They absolutely needed the cash.

Larry had admitted that he and Patty had put their vacation property on the market while they were down there. That had been the real reason for the spur-of-the-moment visit. He'd had to sign the paperwork, get things rolling. He'd told Cooper that he'd made some bad investments and lost a lot of money, but he'd never take anything from his sister.

Stella *really* wanted to believe him.

But who else had access to the piece and knew its value? Stella was certain the frame and photo had been missing since the day she'd returned to town. It hadn't been taken by whoever had torn the living room apart. Which left few options. Or, maybe, many. People liked Beatrice, and she often had visitors.

"I think I might remember them coming," Beatrice murmured, plucking at the lace on her nightgown. "And Karen. She came by this morning."

"That's right."

"And brought me chocolates. Where did they go?"

"You ate them."

"My goodness. I must have been hungry."

"Or you really like chocolate," Trinity said cheerfully.

"I do like chocolate." Beatrice sighed. "I also like home, and I'd really like to go there. I'm sure you can pull some strings, Stella. You're a nurse. Just tell the doctor you'll take care of me. Or have your grandfather do it. I'm sure Henry is anxious for me to come home."

"Nana," Stella began, but she couldn't get the rest of the words past the lump in her throat.

How many times would she have to tell her grandmother the truth? That the man she'd loved for sixty years was gone? That he wasn't waiting at the house for her return? That he would never tell a silly joke or compliment her cooking ever again? How many times would she have to see the tears fill Beatrice's eyes? How many times would she have to break her heart?

"Beatrice," Trinity said, pulling a chair over beside the bed and taking a seat. "How about I read you more of *Little Women*?"

"My favorite story," Beatrice replied, but she looked as sad as Stella felt.

Sad because she wasn't going home, or sad because she suddenly remembered the truth?

"While you two do that, I'm going to run some errands," Stella said. She couldn't sit in the room for another minute, listening to her grandmother's favorite book, staring at the gaudy little Christmas tree.

"I'd love some chocolate, if you have time to stop at the shop," Beatrice said. "It's been months since I've had any."

Stella just kissed her cheek and promised chocolate, and then she walked out of the room.

Simon was sitting beside the door, scrolling through something on his phone. He looked up as she walked out, but he didn't ask where she was going. He wasn't the kind of guy to get involved in other people's business. Chance had told him to guard Beatrice; that's what he was going to do.

Which meant that Stella didn't have anyone following her around the hospital. Not that she needed anyone to do that. She wasn't foolish enough to think she was safe. There'd been no progress made in identifying the guy who'd attacked her.

Not Noah.

She was sure of that.

Now that her mind was clear again, she realized Noah was taller, broader and stronger than her attacker. If he'd wanted to kill her, he would have succeeded. It wasn't Larry, either. His alibi had panned out, and he'd passed a lie detector test.

Whoever it was, he hadn't tried again.

Chance thought there was too much man power on the ground, and that the guy would bide his time, strike again when he thought he had a shot at succeeding.

Chance…

She'd been trying not to think about him because she didn't want to focus on how nice it was to have him around. She didn't want to remember the kisses, the promises, the sweet words.

She didn't want to think about what he'd meant when he'd said he didn't plan to walk away.

Because she was falling harder than she'd ever fallen before. Harder than she'd ever thought she could. For a man who spent his life going into dangerous situations and getting people out of them.

Christmas carols were playing over the hospital intercom, and that only added to Stella's bad mood.

"Can't we just skip Christmas this year?" she muttered, yanking open the stairwell door.

"I don't think my niece and nephew would approve," Chance said, behind her. "But you could put together a petition and see if you can get anyone to sign it."

Startled, she turned around to face him, her heart beating double-time, her stomach doing a funny little dance. He looked like he always did. Handsome. Together. Confident. But he hadn't shaved in a couple of days, he'd traded his dress shirt and tie for jeans, flannel and a heavy coat, and he looked like he spent most of his time outside rather than in a boardroom.

"Where'd you come from?" she asked, her pulse still racing. She wanted to chalk up her fast heartbeat to his sudden appearance. But she couldn't. It was from looking into his eyes and seeing the man who'd been with her through the good and bad and everything in between.

For years.

For longer than Daniel had been with her, and that was odd to think about. That she and Chance had known each other for nearly double the amount of time she'd been married.

"I was getting coffee and saw you leaving the room as I got off the elevator." He held up a carryout cup. "I guess Simon didn't mention that I'd be right back. But then, I'm assuming you didn't ask."

"I needed some air," she responded. "I wasn't going far."

"You shouldn't be going anywhere on your own."

"Now I won't have to."

He smiled, and her pulse jumped again, her thoughts flying back to that moment in his SUV, those tender kisses.

"So why the sudden need for air?" he asked, taking her arm as they walked into the stairwell.

"*Little Women*, Christmas, Beatrice mentioning Henry again," she answered honestly. "Take your pick."

"I'd say that the last is the worst."

He nudged his coffee into her hand, and she took a sip. They'd done all of this dozens of times before. Walking together, talking, sharing coffee. It felt different this time. Maybe because he was there to protect her, and she knew it. Maybe because they were on her home territory, close to all the things that she longed for deep down where it mattered most—home, family, love.

"You're right. I hate breaking her heart over and over again."

"You're not breaking it," he reminded her as he pushed open the lobby-level door. "Losing Henry is."

"Semantics, Chance. It all boils down to the same thing. I have to keep reminding her of the one thing she'd love to forget."

"Is there another choice? Could you live with yourself if you lied to her? Let her think that Henry was alive? Kept building her expectation that she was going to see him again?"

She'd thought about that a lot the last couple of days.

She'd asked herself whether or not lying would bring Beatrice comfort or if it would just bring more pain. In the end, she'd decided to stick with what she knew—honesty.

It's what Beatrice would have wanted if she hadn't had Alzheimer's, and it was what Henry would have expected from his only grandchild.

"Right now, I don't know what I could live with. I only know what my grandmother would want—honesty."

"Then don't feel bad about giving it to her."

He took off his coat and draped it around her shoulders, pulling her hair out from under the collar. "How about we go get something to eat?"

"I'm not hungry."

"You haven't been hungry in four days."

"Are you counting?"

"Yes."

"You know how head injuries are," she said as he tucked strands of hair behind her ear and eyed the bump on her temple. She knew how it looked—green and purple and yellow but better than it had been yesterday and the day before that.

"How are the stitches?" he asked, moving around her and parting the hair near her nape. She hadn't bothered looking at the stitches. They itched, and she knew they were healing. That had been enough information to go on.

"Fine."

"You're going to have a pretty little scar, Stella."

"It'll be the perfect complement to all the big ugly ones."

"Your scars aren't ugly. Nothing about you could ever be ugly." He let her hair drop back into place as he adjusted the coat again. She could feel the warmth of his hands near her skin.

And she just stood there and let it all happen.

She didn't brush his hand away or tell him to stop fussing.

She didn't explain that she was perfectly capable of taking care of herself.

She didn't offer a word of protest when his lips brushed hers. A sweet, gentle kiss, and she wanted more because this was Chance and they'd known each other forever, had been there for each other over and over again.

If that wasn't love, she didn't know what was.

But the sweetness of love had always come with the bitterness of loss. She didn't know if she could take what she wanted and not suffer for it. She didn't know if she could lose Chance and survive it.

Kissing Stella was the best thing he'd ever done and probably the biggest mistake he'd made in a long time, but Chance wasn't about to apologize for it. He knew what he wanted. He'd known for a long time. After spending four days thinking about what could have happened if he hadn't shown up at Beatrice's house at just the right time, he'd decided that he'd be a fool to keep skirting around the thing that was between them.

"Chance—" Stella began as he stepped back.

"If you're going to say I shouldn't have done that, forget it."

"I wasn't."

"Then what were you going to say?"

"That…" She shook her head.

"Tell you what, Stella. For once, how about you just be honest with both of us?"

"You want honesty?" She started walking, his coat still around her shoulders. "I'm terrified."

"Of loving me?"

"Of losing you."

"Who says you have to?"

"Life? Experience? I've lost everyone I've ever loved, Chance. Everyone."

"Do you wish you hadn't loved them?" he asked, his heart breaking for her, but his mind clear and sharp and focused. He knew what she needed to hear. Not a bunch of platitudes. The truth, and this was it—love always had risk, and it was always worth it.

"Of course not."

"Then what's to fear?"

"I don't want to be hurt again."

"Neither do I. But when I weigh the risk versus the benefit, I'm all for giving it a try," he responded as they walked past a Christmas tree that had been set up in the lobby. Colored lights twinkled in the branches and brightly wrapped packages were piled beneath it. A few people were hanging ornaments. Others sat on benches and in chairs, talking and laughing as carols continued to be piped through the intercom.

"You're braver than I am."

"And yet, we both face danger every day."

"You know what I mean, Chance," she said quietly, stopping short in front of the doors. "Even if I weren't afraid to risk my heart, the timing isn't right. My grand-mother—"

"Is very happy to know that you've found someone who cares about you. Do you really think she wants to leave you alone when she's gone?"

Her expression tightened, her lips pressing together.

"I'll take your silence as a no, so how about you stop trying to use Beatrice as an excuse?"

"Fine." She shrugged, walking again, her shoulders stiff and straight, her head high.

He followed her into the sunny day, the crisp, cold air cutting through his flannel shirt. He'd strapped his holster beneath it, his Glock loaded and ready.

He opened the SUV door for her, and he wanted to kiss her again, taste the cold winter air on her lips.

Not the time.

Not when they were both upset.

He closed the door and rounded the vehicle, someone at the edge of the lot catching his eye.

Not a man. A woman. Medium height. Light brown hair. Familiar. But the sun was so bright behind her that he couldn't see her face.

She was watching. He felt that.

He wanted to know why.

He opened the door, leaned in.

"See that woman over there?"

Stella nodded. "I noticed her when you closed the door."

"She's watching us. I'm going to ask why."

"Hold on." She grabbed his hand, her fingers cold, her skin rough from years of climbing, shooting and training. "I think it's Karen," she whispered as if she was afraid the woman would hear.

"She was here earlier," he said. He'd looked through

the bag she'd been carrying, and she hadn't been happy about it.

Twenty-two, a nursing student, a hospital volunteer. Active in church. Young and happy and kind. Maybe she thought she was above suspicion.

She was wrong.

He'd done a little digging, found out that she'd moved to town with her father two years ago. No one had actually been able to tell him why.

He figured this was as good a time as any to ask.

"I'm going to talk to her, see why she's still hanging around."

"She does volunteer here," Stella pointed out.

"She has classes. She should be at school."

"You looked at her college schedule?"

"Trinity did."

"I'm not going to ask how she managed that."

"Me, neither, but she printed it out, and I know where Karen should be. I want to know why she's here instead."

"Looks like she's coming this way," Stella responded.

She was right, Karen was walking across the parking lot. Hurrying, really, her narrow frame encased in a long wool coat. She could be carrying a dozen weapons beneath it, and that bothered Chance.

A lot.

"Stay in the car," he said, closing the door and turning to face Karen.

She was smiling.

Of course. He had yet to see her without a wide grin and a cheerful expression.

"Hi, Chance!" she called. "I thought that was you and Stella. I guess I was right."

"I thought you left a couple of hours ago," he responded, and her smile fell away.

"I did, but my afternoon class was canceled, and I

figured I'd get a few more volunteer hours in. Is that a problem?"

"Just a curiosity."

She laughed. "I like what I do. Is that so curious?"

"Not at all." Simple. To the point. Let her do the talking and see where she went with it.

"I want to do mission work overseas. There are several orphanages supported by our church, and I'd like to use my nursing degree to help there."

"That's charitable of you," he said.

Apparently, that wasn't the response she wanted. She frowned.

"It's not about charity. I just have a heart for orphans. Everyone thinks I'm too young to know what I really want. My father wants me to find a nice guy, get married, spend my life trying to…"

Her voice trailed off, and her cheeks went bright red.

"Anyway, I just came over to say hi to Stella." She leaned down, waved through the closed window.

Stella waved back but didn't get out of the vehicle.

Either she was tired or she was cold or she was as worried as Chance was that someone would take a potshot across the parking lot.

"I'm coming by tomorrow to clean Beatrice's room and get things ready for her, okay?" Karen yelled through the glass, and Stella gave her a thumbs-up.

"She might be released early in the morning. It's what she wants," Stella responded, her voice muffled by the glass.

"I can't make it until the evening. I have college singles group at church at seven. I can stop by your place at five and paint her nails. I'll bring her a sandwich from the diner. She'll like that."

"Sounds good. If plans change and she isn't released—"

"I'll bring everything to the hospital. See you then." Karen walked away, not giving Chance a backward glance.

He slid behind the steering wheel and started the SUV, watching in the rearview mirror as Karen walked into the hospital. "She's an interesting kid."

"She's a hard worker."

"I know a lot of hard workers who work hard at being criminals."

"You don't really think she had anything to do with the attack, do you?" she responded, reaching forward to adjust the heat. Her hand was white from cold, her knuckles red.

She did her own volunteering.

She hadn't mentioned it, and he hadn't asked, but he knew. She spent one morning a week in the NICU, holding premature babies while Beatrice attended occupational therapy and craft classes for dementia patients. She'd scrubbed her skin raw to keep from spreading germs.

He grabbed her hand, and she went completely still, her eyes wide in her pale face. She had fine lines near the corners of her eyes and a tiny scar near her left ear. He'd been there when she'd been hit by shrapnel. He knew exactly how she'd looked as blood seeped from the wound while she ran for a helicopter, an injured child in her arms.

They'd saved the kid, but he'd lost a couple of years off his life thinking she'd been severely injured.

"You need some lotion," he said, running his thumb across her knuckles.

"I need answers more," she responded. "So how about we go by the house? I want to look around. When we're done, we can stop and get Beatrice more of her favorite chocolates."

"It might be better if you take a nap once you get to the house."

"No way. Now that my head is clearer, I want to walk through the woods, see if there's anything that will spark my memory and help me figure out who was out there with me."

"You said there might have been two people."

"I know."

"Do you still think that?"

"I don't know what I think. I just know that I have to keep searching until I find what I'm looking for."

"There's a lot I could say about that," Chance murmured as he backed out of the parking space.

"Like what?"

"Maybe what you're looking for is right in front of you?"

She shook her head, strands of bright red hair sliding across her cheeks. "You know that's not what I'm talking about."

"Maybe it should be. God gives us each a certain amount of time. If we're not careful, it will run out, and we won't have gone after what we really wanted."

"My grandfather always used to say that." She smiled, leaning her head back against the seat and closing her eyes.

"I wish I'd had a chance to meet him. From what I've heard, he was a great guy."

"Did you know he was a pastor?" she asked, her eyes still closed as she seemed to be drifting in some long-ago place, some sweet memory. Her lips were curved, her face soft.

"Yes."

"He really believed that God would make something wonderful out of what happened to my family, and he never stopped telling me that I lived because God had great work for me to do."

"You didn't believe him?"

"I had a hard time believing that a God who had great plans would take my whole family from me and then expect me to still keep on going toward whatever wonderful thing was in store."

"I'm sorry."

"Yeah. Me, too."

"But your grandfather was right. Your family is gone, but dozens of other families are together because of the work you do and the passion you have for it. I know that's cold comfort—"

"No." She opened her eyes. "It isn't. I'm older now. I can accept that the tragedy I lived through brought me to a place where I could help other people. I just find it hard to believe that I'm ever going to find the kind of peace that my grandparents had. An easy, nice, lovely life with all kinds of ordinary miracles—babies and kittens and Christmases filled with happiness and laughter."

"Those things are all around you, Stella," he said, because he thought that she'd missed them too often, so busy pursuing the next rescue, the next big victory, that she'd forgotten to look for the little ones.

"Maybe." She turned on the radio, frowning as a carol filled air. "More Christmas songs."

"It *is* the most wonderful time of year," he joked, but Stella didn't seem amused. She sighed, smoothing her hair and rubbing the back of her neck.

"For some people. For me, it just brings back a lot of bad memories."

"You could change that. You could make some good ones."

She said something, but he didn't hear the words. He was glancing in the rearview mirror, eyeing the truck that had just sped out from a side road.

Black. Shiny. Looked like a newer model, and it was coming fast.

"What's going on?" Stella asked, twisting in her seat

and looking out the back window. "That looks like trouble."

"And *that's* an understatement," he muttered, because they were out in the middle of nowhere, the truck speeding toward them, tinted windows keeping him from seeing how many people were in it. The road stretched straight out in front of them, a steep tree-covered hill to the right, a slush-filled ditch to the left. Too deep to try to drive through. He'd bottom out the SUV.

"There's a driveway about a mile from here," Stella said, her voice tense, her hand gripping the back of the seat as she watched the truck career toward them. "On the left. Very hard to see. Look for a giant spruce and a white mailbox. Turn hard when you see it. There's a small bridge that goes over the ditch."

He stepped on the accelerator, focusing his attention on the road and on keeping a distance between the SUV and the truck.

"He's still coming," Stella murmured, pulling her phone from her pocket and calling for help.

That was great.

Except the truck was closing in, and he could see the barrel of a rifle poking out the window.

"Get down!" he shouted as he caught sight of the spruce and the mailbox. He could see a hint of wood planks. Not much of a bridge, but he yanked the wheel to the left, the SUV skidding sideways and bouncing onto wood, then dirt and grass.

The truck sped past, tires squealing as it tried to brake, glass shattering in the back of the SUV. The guy had taken out the back window.

"Keep going!" Stella yelled. "He's turning around."

Chance didn't need the warning. He was already stepping on the accelerator, speeding toward a distant house and, hopefully, a place to take cover.

NINE

"Do you know what's on the other side of the house?" Chance asked, his voice razor-sharp. He was calculating risk, formulating a plan, doing everything he'd done hundreds of times before.

Stella was doing the same.

It was what they'd been trained for, and she didn't feel panic as much as she felt adrenaline flooding through her, clearing the last cobwebs from her concussed brain.

"A field. Probably not enough coverage, though," she responded, her gaze on the truck. The driver had skidded to a stop and turned around, searching for the entrance to the driveway. Going too fast. He'd have to slow down if he was going to find it.

"Is there another access road to the property?"

"No." The driver had slowed, was backing up, probably knowing that they were cornered. Maybe not realizing who he was going up against. Not an elderly woman wandering through the snowy woods, and not an unsuspecting caretaker rushing to find her. Two well-trained operatives who weren't going to be taken out easily.

"Anyone in the house? It looks empty, but I don't want to take chances that we're going to put civilians in the crosshairs of a gunfight."

"The place has been abandoned for years." As a teenager, she'd spent time exploring the house with her friends, walking through the dusty rooms and looking at furniture that had been left behind decades ago. Eventually, the town council had opted to board up the windows and doors to keep the teenage crowd from partying there, but Stella hadn't let that stop her. She'd found a way into the cellar and brought friends there to tell scary stories.

"Any way to get inside?" Chance asked, that edge still in his voice.

"Yes. There's a cellar door in the back. I broke the lock years ago. Unless someone has fixed it, we should be able to get in."

"You called 911. Did you let Simon and Boone know we've got trouble?"

"Yes." She'd texted coordinates to both of them. She didn't have time to check for a response. She was too focused on the truck. The driver had finally found the entrance and was bouncing over the planks that led to the driveway.

"He's in," she said.

"And we're out of sight," Chance replied, pulling around the side of the house and throwing the SUV into Park. "Let's go," he commanded, but she was already moving, jumping out and running to the cellar door.

It was covered with debris—snow and grass and dirt.

She found the handle and tugged, trying to pull it open. She could hear the truck's engine, the swish of tires on grass and dirt. A quarter mile. That's how far it was from the road to the house. A few seconds of driving, and the guy would be there.

Chance grabbed the handle, wrapping his hand over hers and yanking hard. The old door finally gave, swinging up and open.

"Get in!" Chance shouted, nearly shoving her into the cellar. She stumbled down rickety steps, tripped over an old box and fell, sliding on hands and knees across the earthen floor.

Chance scrambled down the stairs behind her, letting the door drop back into place and plunging the cellar into darkness.

"You okay?" he asked, finding her hand and hauling her to her feet.

"Yes."

"Can we get into the house from here?"

"There's a door…"

"Shhhhh." He pressed a finger against her lips, and she froze.

She could hear the truck's engine, the tires on the frozen yard. Then silence, thick and heavy and horrible.

She grabbed Chance's sleeve and led him across the root cellar. She knew the way. She'd been here dozens of times, and she hadn't forgotten. The cellar was ripe with the scent of dirt and decay, the air frigid with winter. Years ago, fruit and vegetables were stored there, old wooden shelves jutting from the walls, still hosting cans of peaches and pears and pickles.

She couldn't see them through the darkness, but she knew they were there. Just like she knew there was a door in the far wall that led to the stairs. She ran her hand along the packed earth until she felt wood. There'd once been a doorknob. Now it was just a hole. She stuck her fingers through and dragged the door inward, the wood scraping against the floor and sending up a cloud of dust that she could feel on her face.

She didn't dare cough.

"Duck," she whispered in Chance's ear, and then she moved through the small opening, felt cement under her feet, smelled must and mildew.

Chance was right behind her. She could feel the warmth

of his chest against her back, feel his hand on her waist and his breath ruffling her hair.

He pulled the door closed, the quiet whoosh of it mixing with another sound. Wood creaking. The cellar door opening?

Faint gray light shone beneath the door, and Stella knew it was filtering in from outside.

She stepped back, pulling Chance with her.

She expected the door to open, and what she wanted more than anything was her Glock. She'd put it in a lockbox on the top shelf of her closet, afraid that Beatrice might find it and hurt herself.

She hadn't had time to retrieve it.

Now she wished she'd made the time.

Fabric rustled, and she knew Chance had pulled out his firearm. She stayed behind him, out of the line of fire, her gaze trained on the sliver of light that seeped under the door.

They moved in sync, still facing the door, still waiting for it to fly open. One step after another across the basement and to the rickety stairs that led to the main level of the house.

She put her weight on the first step, testing to see if it would hold her, then clambered up the rest, anxiety clawing at her stomach, a warning whispering up her spine.

Something was off.

Really off.

She'd expected their pursuer to rush into the basement, gun drawn, bullets flying. Instead, he was still in the cellar.

Doing what?

That's what she wanted to know.

She reached the basement door, tried the knob.

Locked.

"Let me," Chance whispered, the words tickling the

hair near her ear, the sound of them barely carrying over the pulse of blood in her head.

They needed to get out.

She didn't know anything else, but she absolutely knew that.

She eased to the side. Chance squeezed in between her and the wall, his weight bowing the step they were standing on. She took one step down, glancing at the cellar door, that little wedge of light still visible beneath it.

A shadow passed in front of it.

Once. Twice.

She caught a whiff of something sharp and pungent.

Gasoline?

She had about two seconds to realize it before the cellar door went up in flames, fire licking at the wood and devouring it.

Every nightmare she'd ever had was coming true again. The flames. The smell of gasoline. The screams.

She didn't realize they were coming from her until Chance pulled her against his chest, whispered against her ear. "It's okay. I'm going to get us out of here."

She choked down another scream, her throat raw, her hands trembling as she reached around Chance and started banging on the door.

Panicking.

Terrified because she'd lived this before. A different time. A different place. And she'd lost almost everyone she'd loved.

"Stella." Chance grabbed her arms, held them down at her sides, his grip gentle. "Let me do this, okay? Because I can. I just need you to give me a minute. Trust me."

We don't have a minute, she wanted to shout, but the light from the flames had illuminated the basement, and she could see the cement floor, the rotting stairs. She could see Chance, too, everything about him calm.

He wasn't panicking, and she shouldn't, either.

It was a fire.

Which was probably better than a barrage of bullets shot into the dark.

Below, the flames crackled and hissed, spreading along wooden support beams. It wouldn't be long before the entire place went up.

If they weren't out…

She pushed the thought away, tried to push away the terror, too. Beatrice needed her, and giving in to fear wasn't going to save her.

Please, God, she prayed silently, and she wasn't even sure what she was asking for. Safety? Help? Protection?

All of those things?

Chance jiggled the doorknob, a utility tool in hand. Still no panic in his face.

"Chance," she said, her mouth dry with fear as flames crawled across the ceiling, eating away at the beam that supported the upper floor. "We're running out of time."

They *were* running out of time, the old-fashioned lock trickier to pick than newer ones. Tricky. But not impossible.

Chance twisted the utility tool he always carried, fishing around in the lock for the mechanism that would open it. It caught, the knob finally turning, the door flying open.

He grabbed Stella's hand, dragging her into an empty hall. Pictures hung from the walls, all of them too covered with dust for any details to be visible. Not that he had time to stop and look. Smoke billowed up through warped floorboards, swirling into the air and filling his lungs.

Up ahead, the front door stood dark against the lighter-colored walls. The arsonist could be waiting outside, ready to take a shot when the door opened.

Chance didn't think so, though.

The guy was a coward. He'd shot at them through the truck window, then set fire to the basement door rather than follow them into the darkness and risk being ambushed. He'd taken off by now. Chance could almost guarantee it.

Even if he hadn't, there was no choice but to go out the front door. Heading to the back of the house with the fire blazing in the basement would be a fatal mistake.

"The door is boarded up," Stella said, her voice tight and controlled as if she were afraid of falling apart again. She was moving with him, briskly down the hall. No more screams. No more panic. She was terrified, though. He'd seen it in her face and he'd felt a gut-deep need to find the guy who'd done that to her—who'd terrorized her, who'd made her scream and panic and nearly climb through Chance to get away.

He *would* find the guy.

He would make him pay.

First, he needed to get Stella out of the house and away from the fire.

He opened the front door, eyeing the heavy plywood that blocked the opening. Bits of sunlight shone through cracks near the center, and he aimed for that, kicking once and then again. The wood splintered and then gave, cold air sweeping in.

Outside, the day was silent, the snow-speckled driveway crisscrossed with tire marks. No sign of the truck, but Chance could see a Jeep speeding toward them. Trinity's. She'd better not be in it. He'd told her to stay at the hospital and stick with Beatrice.

"Is that Trinity?" Stella asked, her teeth chattering, her body trembling.

"Let's find out." He led her down the stairs, hurrying

her away from the building. The place was old, the structure compromised, fire eating away at the foundation.

It wouldn't be long before the entire thing came down.

If he hadn't gotten the door unlocked, it wouldn't have mattered. They'd have been overtaken by smoke before the house fell. Black clouds billowed from the back of the house, spiraling into the sky. Fueled by old wood and dry weather, the fire continued to grow.

In the distance, sirens were screaming. Police. Fire trucks. Rescue units. Chance had no doubt they were all on the way. Too late. At least as far as the house was concerned. And as far as catching the perp.

The Jeep stopped a hundred yards from the house, pulling off to the side of the driveway and leaving room for the emergency vehicles to get past. Simon hopped out of the driver's seat and jogged toward them.

"The perp?" he asked, and Chance shook his head.

"Gone."

"You're sure?"

"About as sure as I can be before I check things out." He led Stella to the Jeep.

"I want you to wait here," he said. "The sheriff won't be long. Fill him in when he arrives. Simon and I will head around to the back of the house. Make sure the guy really is gone."

"I'm not going to sit on my behind while you two go do the manly work," Stella said, some of the color back in her cheeks, all of the fear gone from her eyes. She looked like herself now—tough, confident, strong.

"This isn't about fair division of labor, Stella," he responded, using the same tone of voice he always did when they were working together. "I want you to fill Cooper in, because you're the witness. Simon isn't. Get in the Jeep."

It was an order.

She knew it.

Knowing her, he was sure she'd take her sweet time deciding if she was going to follow it. They'd been down this road before. Half the time, she won. Half the time, he did.

This time he wasn't playing games.

"I mean it, Stella. Somebody wants you dead, and if he gets his way, Beatrice is going to be on her own, facing down a threat she can't even begin to understand. Get in the Jeep."

Her lips pressed together and her eyes flashed, but she did what he said, sliding into the Jeep and slamming the door. She had her cell phone in hand, and he could see her making a call as he motioned for Simon.

"We're heading to the back of the house. You head left. I'll head right. I think the guy is gone, but play it cautious. And cut a wide swath around the building. The basement is on fire, and the place is going to come down."

Simon gave a quick nod and took off, jogging toward the edge of the yard and then moving in the direction of the back field.

A squad car was racing along the driveway. Chance didn't wait around to see if the sheriff was driving it. He'd given Stella her instructions. Whether she liked them or not, she'd follow them.

He headed around the side of the building, running parallel to a set of tire tracks. The guy had been in a truck and he'd fired a rifle. Chance knew that much.

He needed to know more.

A face would be nice. A name.

Not Noah Ridgewood. Stella's friend had checked out. He was currently staying at a ranch just outside Fort Worth, and he hadn't been happy when HEART member Dallas Morgan had shown up. Or so Dallas had said. He'd been given about two seconds to state his case, and then the door had slammed in his face.

Didn't matter. Dallas had confirmed Noah's whereabouts, and he should be at the hospital in an hour, ready to take over for Boone.

So the perp wasn't Noah, and Chance didn't think Larry was directly responsible for the violence. He was lying low, staying at home and keeping quiet about his troubles. The guy didn't seem capable of hurting anyone. Although it was possible he'd hired someone to do it. He'd taken funds out of his savings account several times over the past year. The amount had added up to just over twenty thousand dollars. He'd told the sheriff that he'd been using it to pay off debts that he'd accrued, but there'd been no trace of the money. No cashed checks. No deposits. It had been there and then it was gone.

Which could mean a lot of things.

Could mean he had some bad habits—gambling, drugs, women. Could mean he owed the wrong people money and had paid it back in cash.

It didn't necessarily mean that he'd hired a hit man to take out his sister and niece.

But it also didn't mean that he hadn't.

The backyard was empty, just like Chance had expected. No truck. No gunman. Just his SUV parked too close to the house. Too late to move it. The fire had spread across the back facade and had set several shrubs ablaze.

He could see the area where the truck had been parked, the packed snow and crushed grass. Smudges of gray from the exhaust. A few feet away, an old gas canister and a lighter lay abandoned, half hidden by snow. Chance crouched in front of them.

"What did you find?" Simon asked beside him.

"Looks like the accelerant. We'll have to have the local PD look for prints."

"If the guy set the place ablaze with gasoline and a lighter, he's an idiot."

"I'd say he soaked the door with gasoline, lit a piece

of cloth or paper and tossed it. He'd have a pretty good chance of igniting the gas that way, and he'd avoid going up in flames himself."

"Guy is still an idiot. He's not going to get away with this."

"He already did."

"You know what I mean, Chance." Simon straightened. "We're going to find him, and we're going to make him really sorry."

"Law enforcement will hand out the consequences," Chance reminded him. "But you're right. We are going to find him."

"Chance!" Sheriff Brighton strode toward them, his expression grim and hard. "You need to clear out. Fire crews are moving in."

"We've got a gas canister here. A lighter."

"I'll have one of my men collect it. Right now, we want all civilians clear."

Chance wasn't going to argue.

One thing he'd learned early in his career—get on the good side of local law enforcement, play by their rules and you might just get a favor when you needed one.

"Did you see Stella?" he asked, and Cooper nodded.

"I have a deputy questioning her. She gave a description of the vehicle. Dark truck. Newer model. Ford or Chevy."

"That's right."

"I spotted one parked on the side of the road on my way here. Looked like one of the tires was blown."

"You stop to check it out?"

"I was in a hurry to save your hide. So, no. I'm going back there now."

"Mind if I come along? I'll know if it's the right vehicle."

"As long as you keep your distance, keep your hands off the evidence and don't ask questions."

"I can manage that," he responded.

"We'll see," Cooper muttered as he led the way to his squad car.

TEN

Midnight, and Chance hadn't returned to the hospital.

Stella had been back for hours, clean clothes on, chocolate in hand, every trace of smoke washed from her skin and hair. She'd been back to the house, gotten the things she needed. She'd smiled at Beatrice, listened to her talk about Henry and their wedding and the beautiful life they'd lived together. For a while, it had seemed like she remembered it all. The years they'd spent loving each other, the wonderful home they'd shared, even his death.

Eventually, she'd asked to go home, and then she'd asked why Henry hadn't visited, and the whole cycle of grief began again. She'd cried herself to sleep, and Stella had wanted to cry with her. She hadn't because it would only have upset Beatrice more.

She still wanted to cry.

The fire had been too much.

After everything else—Granddad's death, her return to Boonsboro, the nightmares, the attacks—it seemed like the last straw. For the first time in longer than she could remember, she wanted to throw in the towel and call it quits.

"Everything okay in here?" Boone peeked in the open door, a cup of coffee in one hand and a pretzel in the other.

"Have you heard from Chance?"

"Not yet, but Dallas finally arrived. I'm going to be heading home in a minute. Just thought I'd ask if you needed anything before I go."

"I need to speak with Chance."

"Sorry, I can't help you with that." He smiled and took a bite of the pretzel.

"Boone, do you ever stop eating?" Trinity asked groggily. She'd been sleeping in the chair, head on her knees, doing exactly what her brother had asked. As far as Stella knew, she hadn't left Beatrice's side all day.

"Not if I can help it. Got a couple of these babies from the cafeteria a few hours ago. They're just as good cold as they were warm. You want one?"

"No. Simon brought me a sandwich a couple of hours ago." Trinity yawned and stood. "You said Dallas is here?"

"Should be on the elevator up."

"I guess he found out what he wanted to know."

"What did he want to know?" Stella asked, and Trinity blushed.

"Nothing."

"If it's nothing, why do you look like you just spilled top secret information?"

"I—"

"Tell you what," Boone said. "I'm going to leave you two to figure this all out. I'm heading to the elevator. As soon as Dallas gets off, I'm getting on. Got a wife and some kids who are missing me." He took another bite of his pretzel and walked away.

"Well?" Stella demanded, keeping her voice low enough not to wake Beatrice.

"Well what?"

"What was Dallas doing that I'm not supposed to know about?"

"He went to talk to Noah."

"Wonderful." She snagged her phone from the table

near Beatrice's bed. No messages. No angry texts. Whatever had happened, Noah seemed willing to let it drop. "We've been friends for years. I told your brother—"

"What did you tell me?" Chance asked, walking into the room. He looked tired—his eyes shadowed, his hair mussed—and all her irritation slipped away. She wanted to tell him to sit down, ask him if he'd eaten, get him a hot cup of coffee and a warm blanket.

More than anything, she wanted to pull him into her arms and kiss him. She forced the thought from her mind.

"It's not important."

"It was important enough five seconds ago," Trinity muttered.

"Tell you what, sis," Chance said, his gaze on Stella. "How about you take a break? I'm sure Stella wouldn't mind you spending the night at her grandmother's place. The sheriff is running patrols by there every few minutes, you'll be safe enough."

"A real bed?" Trinity perked up, her blue eyes bright with happiness. "Are you serious?"

"You've worked three days without a break. Now that Dallas is here, you need to get some rest. Come back in the morning, and we'll set you up with Beatrice again."

"Do you mind?" Trinity asked, and Stella shook her head.

"Here's the key." She dug it out of her purse and handed it to Trinity. "Use any of the bedrooms. If you want clean linens—"

"All I want is a bed. And maybe a pillow. I'll see you in the morning." She took off without a backward glance.

"Maybe she's finally cured," Chance said.

"Of what?"

"Her desire to go on missions."

She snorted. "Not hardly. She'll be back in the morning, armed for bear."

He smiled at that, crossing the distance between them in two long strides.

He was right there, in her space, and she didn't move back, just reached up and smoothed his hair, let her hand settle on his shoulder. His coat was cold and damp as if winter had soaked into it, and everything about him was so right and so wonderfully familiar. She wanted so badly to believe that what they had could last. That she could give herself over to love and not be sorry for it.

"You look tired," she said. "And cold."

"I'm both. The truck Cooper spotted? It was the one that chased us down."

Her pulse jumped, hope springing to life. If they'd found the truck, they might have found the perp. "Were you able to find the driver?"

"He was long gone, and the truck was reported stolen yesterday, so we can't trace him through that. We found something, though."

"What?"

"An old Remington 22. A long rifle. Probably from the early twentieth century. Same caliber as the bullet that was found in the SUV."

"That's an odd weapon to choose."

"It certainly isn't a common one. What's interesting is that the knife was old, too. An old bowie knife. Probably close to a hundred years old. At least, that's what the expert Cooper hired said."

"An antiques buff?" she asked, surprised by the information and intrigued by it.

"Sounds like it. Or like someone who has access to antiques. Ring any bells?"

She wished it did, but she shook her head. "None. Is Cooper checking the serial number on the rifle? Maybe—"

"It's too old."

"So we've still got nothing to go on."

"We've got the rifle, we have the knife and we have a lighter the guy dropped. Cooper pulled a print off it. He's running it through the database, trying to get a match."

"Was he able to get any prints from my place?"

"A couple of partials. He said he was going to come by tomorrow to get Beatrice's prints and yours. Anyone else who has spent a lot of time in your house?"

"Just Karen."

"He'll have to get hers, too."

"I'll text her and let her know." She grabbed her phone and typed a quick message. "She's supposed to stop by the house tomorrow evening. Maybe he can just come there."

"You think Beatrice is going to be ready to go home."

"I hope she is." She walked to the bed, touched her grandmother's forehead. She felt warm, her cheeks pink.

Too many blankets? Or a fever?

Concerned, she checked Beatrice's pulse. A little rapid, but steady.

"What's wrong?" Chance asked, and she shook her head.

"I'm probably worrying about nothing."

"You never worry about nothing. What's wrong?"

"She feels warm. Or maybe I'm just cold."

Chance's hand settled on Beatrice's brow, his skin tan against her pallor. "She does feel warm. Why don't you call a nurse? Have her vitals taken. If nothing else it will give you peace of mind."

"Peace of mind," Beatrice murmured, her eyes opening.

Did they look glassy?

Or was that Stella's imagination, too?

"If you take a piece of my mind, I won't have any left. I've already lost too many of my marbles," she continued, and Chance chuckled, his hand dropping away.

"You're as funny as your granddaughter, Ms. Beatrice."

"Call me Nana. All my family does."

"We're not family, but I'll be happy to call you Nana."

"We're not family *yet*," Beatrice said with a sly smile.

"Nana—" Stella began, but Beatrice coughed, the wheezy rasp alarming. "Are you okay?"

She grabbed the pitcher of water, poured some into cup and handed it to Beatrice.

"I'm fine. Just still a little under the weather. Maybe it was the chocolates I ate. They tasted funny."

"You said they were delicious earlier," she reminded her. "Hopefully, your pneumonia isn't getting worse."

"Do I have pneumonia?"

"Yes, but you're on the mend."

"That's good, dear. Now let's talk about the wedding."

"What wedding?"

"Yours. I have my mother's wedding dress packed in a box in the attic. It will look lovely on you."

"Nana," she said gently, "I'm not even engaged."

"Yet," Beatrice said, her gaze shifting to Chance. "Christmas is the perfect time for an engagement. Don't you think?"

"I think that Christmas is the perfect time for just about anything," he responded.

Not quite, Stella wanted to say. With all the bad memories and nightmares so tied to the holiday, she didn't think she'd ever be able to enjoy it. For Beatrice's sake, she'd have to try.

"I knew I liked you, young man," Beatrice murmured, her eyes drifting closed again, her face going slack. Awake and then asleep. That didn't seem right to Stella. Sure, it was late. Sure, Beatrice had had a rough few days, but she'd been her usual spunky and energetic self the past two days.

This seemed like a setback.

She pushed the call button for the nurse, felt Beatrice's forehead again.

"Hovering isn't going to help her get better," Chance said, dropping into a chair. His long legs stretched out in front of him, his shoes speckled with mud. She'd forgotten how tired he'd looked, forgotten how cold he'd been.

She took a blanket from the end of Beatrice's bed and tucked it around his shoulders.

"You were outside for too long," she chided, and he smiled.

"I think we both know that I've spent way more time outside in the cold and survived it."

"I think we both know that I need someone to fuss over. It might as well be you." She moved away, though, because she shouldn't be so close. Shouldn't be tempting herself so much.

"Come here." He snagged her hand, tugging her so close that their knees were touching, and something warm and wonderful welled up in the region of her heart. Something filled with sweetness and beauty. Something she'd never really looked for and hadn't ever expected to find.

She should pull away.

She knew she should.

She should guard her heart, because she was going to get hurt again. She'd never ever wanted this kind of love. The kind that consumed everything, filled every empty spot in her heart.

Even during her marriage, she hadn't looked for it. She'd loved Daniel. She had, but she'd known that she couldn't count on him to be there for her. Not for birthdays or holidays. Not for funerals or weddings. She'd planned every life event knowing that she'd probably be alone because Daniel's work demanded all of his time and energy and commitment, and there hadn't been anything left for her.

And that had been fine.

It was the way she'd wanted it.

It wouldn't be that way with Chance.

She knew it.

And it terrified her.

"I was worried about you earlier," he said. "I've never seen you so scared."

"You've never seen me scared," she corrected, her voice tight from the memory of those flames lapping at the door, the smoke pouring into the basement.

"Was it the fire?" He ignored the comment, his hands settling on her waist.

"Did I ever tell you that I can remember it all? The accident I was in?"

"No."

"It was Christmas day, and we'd just been to my grandparents' house. My sisters and I were all sitting in the backseat of the old car my dad drove, and I was holding the gift my grandparents had given me. A copy of *Little Women*. Only it wasn't an ordinary copy. It was old with beautiful watercolor illustrations inside."

"You don't have to talk about this, Stella," he said, but she did have to because Chance deserved more than the little pieces of herself that she was always giving, he deserved more than the tiny glimpses of her heart that she allowed others to see.

"I think I do. I think you deserve to know. I'm sure you *do* know." She laughed, the sound harsh and painful. "Some of it anyway. You do background checks on all your employees. I know you read the newspaper reports about the accident."

He didn't deny it, just watched her through those deep blue eyes, his hands still on her waist.

"My sister and I were bickering because she wanted to touch the illustrations in the book. Eva was six years younger than me, and she was always tearing up papers and scribbling on things." She could remember that, just like she could remember Eva's dark brown eyes, her pretty smile, her soft red hair.

She blinked, surprised at the sting of tears in her eyes.

"I don't think my parents even saw the truck that hit us. The guy had been drinking all night, and he was probably going seventy in a thirty-miles-an-hour zone. He lost control and hit us head-on. One minute, my life was normal and happy. The next, flames were everywhere. The window beside me had shattered, and I managed to unbuckle my seat belt. I could see my parents, and…I knew they were dead. My baby sister was gone, too, but Eva was alive. At least, I thought she was, and I couldn't leave without her."

Her voice broke, and Chance was up, wrapping his arms around her, pressing her head to his chest.

"I couldn't save her," she said, the words muffled. "I was trying so hard to get her seat belt unbuckled, and my shoulder was burning, my hair was on fire, and I didn't want to leave her, but some man…some guy dressed like Santa…yanked me through the window, and I didn't have a choice."

Her arms slid around him, her hands clutching his shirt. She wanted to burrow deeper into his arms, disappear into the comfort of his embrace, let all the horrible memories be chased away and replaced by better ones.

"If there is one thing I know, Stella, it's this," he responded. "If it had been possible to save your family, you would have done it. I also know that, while you've spent years focusing on the tragedy, your grandparents focused on the gift they received. They could have lost everyone. Instead, you were pulled from the wreck and returned to them. That's amazing. I'd say they spent every day after that Christmas thanking God for it."

She'd never thought of that.

But maybe she should have.

All these years that she'd wondered why her grandparents still loved Christmas, all the times when she'd wondered how they could stand to put up a tree, sing the old carols, go to church and thank God for His gifts, and she'd never thought that she was one of the gifts they had been most thankful for.

She glanced at the tree that Trinity had brought, thought about how happy Beatrice had been to see it. Not just a symbol of Christmas but of grace and mercy.

"I'm going to have to dig the stockings out of the attic," she said, and Chance smiled.

"I'll help you," he said, his lips brushing her forehead, her cheek, her mouth.

He lingered there, and she was lost, all the memories and nightmares gone, the longing for home and family and love taking their place.

Someone knocked on the door, and Chance broke away, his pulse racing wildly. He wanted to hold on to Stella, to keep her close, but she moved away, her hand shaking as she pressed her palm to Beatrice's forehead as a nurse walked in.

She was worried.

Chance couldn't blame her. Beatrice was pallid, her cheeks gaunt, her body frail. She'd faded since he'd seen her at the funeral, and even then she'd been fragile.

Stella explained the situation to the nurse, her voice shaking. Maybe from nerves or maybe from the aftermath of the kiss. He didn't ask. Wouldn't ask. There were more important things to think about. More important things to worry about.

For now.

Later, they'd talk about it again.

"She does feel a little warm," the nurse confirmed, taking out a thermometer and running it across Beatrice's forehead. "Ninety-nine point eight. Not too bad. I'm going to make a note of this and call the attending physician."

She pressed a stethoscope to Beatrice's chest, and the older woman shifted in her sleep. "Sounds clear, but I think I hear bronchial wheezing."

"Are you going to check her oxygen levels?" Stella asked.

"I know how to do my job, ma'am." The nurse offered a tight smile as she attached a sensor to Beatrice's finger. "She seems to be sleeping deeply. Is that normal for her?"

"Not usually." Stella touched Beatrice's cheek. "Nana?"

Beatrice moaned but didn't open her eyes.

"Oxygen levels are at 90. So that's good. I'm going to call the doctor, though. We'll see what he says. He may want to order some blood work. Maybe run an X-ray. Hold tight. If anything changes, buzz me."

"I should call my great-uncle and let him know what's going on," Stella murmured as the nurse walked away.

"I'm not sure Larry needs to be informed of anything."

"We don't know what he's involved in, but the lie detector test—"

"Can be cheated."

"He loves Beatrice, Chance," she said, her hair mussed from their kiss, her lips still pink. She was a beautiful woman. He'd always thought that. Over the years, he'd seen just how deep that beauty went. Her attention to her grandmother, her need to make sure she was okay, her desire to believe her uncle—it was all part of that beauty, and Chance wouldn't try to change it.

"Call him. If he comes, we'll keep an eye on things."

"And maybe we'll ask him a few questions," she responded. "He did give that money to someone, and I do think that's the key to all of this." She met his eyes. "When

I say *we'll* ask questions, I mean *I'll* ask questions. My great-uncle is older, and—"

"Make the call, Stella." He cut her off because he wasn't going to make any promises. He'd seen Larry a couple times, but the guy had scurried in and out, staying as far away from Chance as possible.

Because of what had happened at Beatrice's house?

Or because he was hiding something and was afraid that Chance would uncover it?

One way or another, Chance was going to discover the truth. Stella and her grandmother had been through a lot, and they deserved a little peace.

He touched the Christmas tree.

Stella had been right. He'd known the bare basics of her story. He'd read the articles. He knew about the drunk driver, the crash, the fire, the broken window, the father of three who'd been playing Santa for his kids when he'd heard the crash.

He knew that Stella's Christmas dress had been on fire when she'd been yanked from the wreck, that the man who'd saved her had been sure she was going to die because her body was broken, her skin peeling from her arm and shoulder, but he'd run with her into his house, laying her on the wood floor, covering her with a blanket, handing her a little stuffed toy one of his kids had abandoned—all while the car with her family in it burned.

Yeah. He'd read all that.

But he'd never heard the hitch in Stella's voice. He'd never seen the pain in her eyes, the regret and sorrow and heartbreak. He'd never heard her tell the story in her own words, with all the details of the moments before and the moments after.

He'd only heard her cry out in her dreams, and now he knew what the nightmare was, knew exactly what chased her from sleep.

He couldn't change it.

He couldn't make it different than what it was.

He couldn't ease the pain of loss or protect her from losing someone else, but he could be there for her. He could make the way a little easier. He could offer the best of himself and hope that it filled some of the holes in her life, made the empty spots less painful.

If she let him.

For now, he'd do what he knew—his job.

Three times, someone had tried to kill Stella. If she were a different kind of person, she'd be dead. He could assume that the assassin didn't know her background or her training. First, he'd come after her in the woods. Then in the hospital. Both times, he'd used the element of surprise, but he'd been willing to go hand to hand with her. Maybe assuming that a woman would be easy to overpower.

The third time, he'd taken the coward's way—avoiding direct contact.

He was learning from his mistakes, and that could make him even more dangerous.

He was also using some very odd weapons.

Not a handgun or a typical hunting rifle. A Remington 22. Antique. Same for the bowie knife. It had been handcrafted in the 1800s.

Stella had said she didn't know anyone involved in the antiques trade, but she'd been busy since she'd returned to Boonsboro. Caring for Beatrice had become her job. He'd been calling weekly since she'd arrived, and she always had a list of therapies she had to bring Beatrice to, doctor's appointments. Hair. Nails. Little outings to keep Beatrice happy and engaged.

He met her eyes, realized she'd been watching him, her hand still on Beatrice's cheek, her eyes still filled with all the memories she'd shared.

"We're going to figure this out," he said.

"I know."

"And then we're going to find those stockings, and we're going to hang them on the fireplace mantel, and we're going to give your grandmother the best Christmas she's had in years."

"We?"

"Why not?" he responded. "Unless you'd rather go it alone."

"I've been going it alone for a while," she said. "I don't think I know how to do anything else."

"You can learn."

"I can also lose. Again. Don't make me rehash it all, Chance, just so you can understand why I can't think of Christmas and family and gifts and fun." She swallowed hard, and he knew she was fighting tears.

When she turned away, he let her.

He wouldn't push her.

Wouldn't beg her.

He'd offered what he had.

It would be enough or it wouldn't.

Either way, he was there for her.

"I'm going to talk to Dallas and Simon," he said. "There's something about the choice of weapons that's bothering me. This guy has to have access to antiques."

"You know what I've been thinking about?" she asked, obviously relieved by the switch in topics. "The frame that's missing. Not many people would know how much it was worth. *I* just thought it was a gaudy little bauble, and I lived in that house for years. Whoever took it had to have knowledge enough to know what he was taking."

"So we're back to the antiques angle."

"I'm going to ask my uncle to stop by the house tomorrow. I want him to see if anything else is missing. There are a lot of valuables in the house, and he has probably kept a record of them."

"You think he's the right person to ask?"

"I think that he's the only person who will know if something is missing. Beatrice…" She shook her head. "He's the only one."

"Ask him, then. I'll have Trinity and Simon stay here. We'll supervise Larry's visit to the house. Dallas can help us with that."

"I don't think—"

"Let me do this my way, okay? My heart isn't involved. Not in the way that yours is." It was involved, though. With her. With wanting the best outcome, the best ending.

With wanting to make good on his promise that everything was going to be okay.

She hesitated, her gaze dropping back to Beatrice and then returning to him. "Fine. We'll do it your way, but don't expect my acquiescence to become a habit."

He laughed, opening the door and stepping out into the hall. Dallas and Simon were waiting there, one sitting in the chair, the other leaning against the wall. Both newer to the team. Both as hard-core and well-trained as anyone.

A good team. A ready team.

The guy who was after Stella?

He'd made a big mistake going up against a member of HEART. He probably didn't realize that yet, but he would.

Chance was going to make certain of it.

ELEVEN

Beatrice's fever got worse overnight and, by seven in the morning, her cheeks were pink, her eyes glassy. She seemed in good spirits and even managed to eat one of the chocolates, but Stella was concerned. So was Larry. He'd stayed at the hospital through the night, pacing the small room and driving Stella nearly insane with his worry.

She thought Larry was driving Chance insane, too. He'd taken a seat near the door, his long legs stretched out in front of him, his arms crossed over his chest. He'd asked Larry a few questions, but Larry had brushed off the interrogation, his focus on Beatrice.

Either Chance had wanted to keep the peace, or he hadn't believed Larry had anything else to offer. Either way, he'd retreated to the chair an hour ago and had been sitting there silently ever since. She should have been able to ignore him, but that had proved impossible. Even in his silence he was a loud presence in her life.

She'd found her eyes drawn to him again and again. Found herself moving in his direction more than once.

She'd stayed way, because she needed to.

She couldn't do Christmas and family and stockings and gifts, and she didn't want to keep him from having all those things. She cared too much, loved too much to ever be the one to make him miserable.

"You'd think they'd have come to get her for the X-rays already," Larry muttered for what seemed like the fiftieth time. He was sitting next to the bed, his shoulders stooped, his hair uncombed.

"Who is having an X-ray?" Beatrice asked, and Larry patted her hand.

"You are, sis."

"Am I sick?"

"I certainly hope not." He smiled, and Stella saw the gentleness of his expression, the kindness in his eyes. He loved his sister. He'd never hurt her.

Not for money. Not for anything.

"Me, too, because I'm ready to go home." Beatrice looked around and frowned. "Where's the girl?"

"Girl?" Stella asked. "Karen, you mean?"

"Not Karen. She and I don't see eye to eye. It's the other one that I like."

"Since when do you and Karen not get along?" Stella asked, surprised by Beatrice's comment. Karen had been working for Beatrice before Stella arrived—cleaning the house every Monday and Thursday, taking her to the store when Henry couldn't. At least, that's what Larry had told her when he'd recommended that Stella keep Karen on as a part-time home care aide.

"Since the day she walked into my house," Beatrice responded. "Now Henry? He thought she was wonderful, and who was I to argue with your grandfather. The man had the softest heart." She closed her eyes and smiled, caught in some long-ago memory.

"Nana," Stella prodded, "why didn't you tell me you didn't like Karen?"

"Of course she likes Karen. Of course you like her," Larry cut in. "You've told me she's a great housekeeper and a good driver."

"And nosy. I don't like people digging around in my

home." Beatrice frowned. "What were we talking about, dear?"

"Karen?" Stella said.

"Right. She's a hard worker, but the other girl reads to me. What's her name? Charlie?"

"Trinity?" Stella offered.

"That's it! Trinity. She's a lovely girl. Where is she?"

"At the house. She'll be back soon."

"Maybe she can bring Henry when she comes. Do I have her number? I'll call her and tell her to bring him."

Larry looked stricken, his eyes watery, his cheeks pale. "Beatrice—"

"Remember that game we used to play when we were kids, Larry?"

"Which game was that?"

"The one with the flashlights. You'd make all those little animals with your hands. You always were the clever one out of the two of us, and I never could figure out why Dad left me the house."

"Because he'd already bought me a place, remember?" he responded gently. "I got married, and he bought me that house in town. It seemed only right that you and Henry have the family home. Besides, you always loved it more than I did."

"If I don't ever get back there—" she began, but Stella couldn't listen to it.

"You're going to get back there, Nana. Soon. You just need to get a little better. That's all."

"You can't know what tomorrow will bring, sweetie. If I don't get back there, it's yours. You know that, right? I want you to fill it with happiness. Just the way your grandfather and I did. Just the way your parents would have when we handed it over to them. You know that was our gift to them that Christmas, right?"

"What are you talking about?"

"We had that wonderful Christmas lunch together, and Henry and I told your mother and father that the house was going to be theirs." She was crying, tears sliding down her cheeks.

Stella wiped them away, tears burning her own eyes and clogging her throat. She wouldn't let them fall, because Beatrice needed her to be strong.

"Nana, you and Henry were the best parents anyone could ask for, and I love you for it, but I'm not going to listen to any more talk about me inheriting the house. We're going to live there together for a long time before that ever happens."

"She's right, sis," Larry cut in, pouring water into a cup and handing it to Beatrice. "You've got many more years ahead of you. A lot of good years. You'll see."

"And Christmas is coming." Beatrice wiped at the last of her tears, offered a watery smile that made Stella's heart hurt even more. "I love Christmas. Are you hosting a party this year, Larry?"

The two began discussing parties and Christmas and family, and Stella tried to listen, to contribute, to act cheerful. Inside, she still wanted to cry. Mostly because seeing her grandmother lying in a hospital bed, her hold on reality tenuous, was as painful as remembering the accident.

"You okay?" Chance asked.

"I will be."

"Trinity is on her way. I texted her." He leaned close, his lips against her ear as he whispered, "I don't think I can take another second of your uncle's pacing or worrying." The confession surprised a laugh out of her, and Larry glanced their way, frowning.

"You're standing a little close to my niece, young man," he snapped. "How about you go out in the hall and wait there?"

"How about we both go out in the hall? I have a few questions I'd like to ask you."

"You already asked me plenty. So has the sheriff. I've answered them all, and I'm not in the mood to answer again."

"Where did you meet Karen?" Chance asked, the question as surprising to Stella as it seemed to be to Larry. His mouth opened. Closed.

"What do you mean, where did I meet her?" he hedged, and every nerve in Stella's body jumped to attention.

Karen.

She'd been knit into the fabric of Beatrice's life before Stella returned to Boonsboro. She had a key to the house. She had full access to every room in it. She cleaned and polished and ran errands. Stella hadn't thought much about that when she'd arrived. She'd been too concerned about Beatrice, too focused on dealing with Henry's death. Karen had just been a side note in the drama that had been unfolding.

Only maybe she wasn't a side note.

That's what Chance was thinking. She could see it in his face—the grim set of his jaw, the hardness in his eyes.

"It's a simple question, Larry. You met her somewhere. I'd like to know where."

"Church," he rushed to say, but the damage was done. He'd already taken too long, and Stella wanted to know why.

"When Trinity gets here, we're going to the house, Uncle Larry," she said, "you can come with us. I want to see if anything besides the picture frame is missing."

"What frame?" Beatrice asked, and Stella wished she'd kept quiet.

"Just one of the ones on the mantel. I was looking for it."

Beatrice seemed satisfied with that answer, but Larry looked…

The only way to describe it was sick.

"I'd rather stay with my sister. She needs someone looking out for her best interests."

"Don't worry," Chance said. "I'll have people here to make sure she's okay."

"I'd rather—"

"You're coming to the house, Larry," Chance said. "If you don't, I'm going to wonder why."

That was it.

Larry pressed his lips together and didn't say another word.

Maybe Larry *had* met Karen at church, but it seemed odd that a man his age would make such a quick connection with a college student. If his wife had been the one to suggest that Beatrice and Henry hire the young woman, Stella might have believed the story. As it was, things didn't make sense.

That bothered her. A lot.

She eyed her uncle. He was a nice-looking man. Still fit and handsome, despite his advanced age. Was it possible he and Karen...

No way.

There was no way the two had been having an affair. Was there?

If they were, that might explain the missing money, the nervousness that Larry exhibited every time his financial situation came up.

It might also explain the attacks.

With Beatrice and Stella out of the way, there'd be nothing to prevent Larry from giving Karen everything she might want. Money, expensive things. Was it possible that's what the young woman wanted? Could she be the one responsible for luring Beatrice outside, for attacking Stella?

No. The person with the knife had been a man. Stella was certain of that.

But…

Karen. Yeah. She might be the piece of the puzzle that had been missing. If Stella could figure out who she was and what she wanted, she just might find the answers she'd been looking for.

After too many hours watching Larry pace the room, worry over his sister and avoid answering questions, Chance was ready to shake the truth out of the guy. Despite his obvious affection for Beatrice and Stella, it was clear he was hiding something. Whatever it was, it was wearing him down. Even Chance could see that.

He wanted to know what it was.

Something that had to do with Karen?

Maybe.

Chance texted Trinity and requested that she run a full background check on the young woman. Sure, she'd looked at Karen's class schedule, confirmed how long she'd been in town, found her address, but she hadn't run her photo through HEART's face-match program. It was possible Karen had changed her identity before moving to Boonsboro. It was possible she wasn't the person she was claiming to be.

Twenty minutes later, Trinity walked into the room, her computer in one hand, a cup of coffee in the other and a huge duffel bag tossed over her shoulder.

"What's the word?" she asked, going straight to Beatrice's bed. "I hear you've got a fever and won't be going home."

"That's what they tell me. A clever girl like you could probably find a way to sneak me out."

"Probably, but I want you healthy, so I did something better." She put the duffel on the bed and unzipped it. "Christmas stuff! I found the stockings in your attic. I also found some really cool old Christmas cards. Let's hang them on the door. We'll make this place festive for as long as you're in it."

"I told them," Beatrice said, beaming. "I told them you were wonderful."

"Did you?" Trinity pulled out a pile of cards. "How about you look through these, Beatrice? Just to make sure there aren't any that are really special to you."

"Call me Nana," Beatrice responded. "All my family does."

"I'd tell you to call me what my family does, but generally, my siblings call me brat, so we'll just stick with my given name."

Beatrice chuckled, her gnarled fingers thumbing through cards that looked to be decades old. "These are all before my time. My mother just loved to collect things. Perhaps we won't hang them since they're so old."

"I can take them back to the house, if you'd like, Nana," Stella said. "While you and Trinity decorate, I'm going to make a quick trip home."

"Bring me a sandwich when you come back, will you, dear?" Beatrice asked, handing the cards back to Stella and accepting a kiss on her cheek.

"Of course. I'll bring you a fresh nightgown, too."

"And my pink kneesocks. The ones you bought me. They're my favorite." She inhaled deeply, and Chance thought he heard a quiet rattle in her lungs.

"Maybe I should stay," Stella said, and Beatrice gestured her away.

"Of course you shouldn't. I'm perfectly fine, and Trinity and I have Christmas plans to make. I haven't gotten my shopping done. You don't mind helping me with that, do you, dear?" she asked.

"Not at all. We can make a list, and I'll go out later. After Stella returns."

"Come on," Chance said, cupping Stella's elbow. "Standing over the bed worrying isn't going to change anything, so we may as well proceed with the plan."

"You're right," she agreed. "And the sooner we go, the sooner we can return. Come on, Uncle Larry."

"I'd prefer to stay here."

"I don't think you were given that option," Chance said, and Larry blanched.

"Are you threatening me?"

"I don't make threats. I act," Chance responded, walking out into the hall with Stella.

Larry followed. Just like Chance knew he would.

"I don't know what you're thinking," he sputtered, his gaze jumping to Dallas who'd moved into step beside them. "But whatever it is, you're wrong."

"I'm looking for answers. I think you might have them." Chance led the group to the stairwell, motioning for Dallas to move ahead.

"Answers to what? Why Stella was attacked? If you think I have anything to do with that—"

"You want to know what I think, Uncle Larry?" Stella asked quietly, her words barely carrying over the sound of their footfalls.

"You know I do, honey." Larry took her hand. "You're as important to me as any of my own children or grandchildren. You know that, right? I'd never do anything to hurt you."

"That's what I think. That you wouldn't hurt me or Beatrice, but that someone you know might."

"What are you talking about?"

They'd stepped into the lobby, and Dallas jogged outside to get the car.

"Who is Karen?" Stella asked.

"I already told you. We met at church."

"I don't believe you."

"I'm not a liar."

"Are you a cheat?" Stella responded.

"How can you say something like that?" he asked, his cheeks flaming red.

"You're not denying it," Chance pointed out, and the older man shot him a look filled with anger.

He didn't say a word, though. Not as Dallas pulled up in front of the doors. Not as Chance hurried Stella to the SUV. Not as he climbed in beside her.

Dallas took Larry's arm, ushered him around to the front passenger seat.

"Get in," he ordered, and waited impatiently while Larry did so.

Still not a word from Stella's uncle.

"Well?" Stella demanded. "You were going to answer my question, Larry. Weren't you?"

No uncle this time, and Chance was certain Larry noticed.

They pulled away from the hospital entrance and onto the highway, the seconds ticking by, Larry's breathing harsh and a little hitched. He'd gone from bright red to stark white, and Dallas must have noticed. He put a hand on Larry's arm.

"Calm down, Granddad. Nothing is going to be fixed if you drop dead."

"I'm not your granddad," Larry muttered. "And if you think I had an affair with a little girl who is young enough to be my great-granddaughter, you can think again, Stella. Patty is everything to me, and I couldn't bear the thought of hurting her."

"People cheat," Dallas cut in, taking over the questioning, playing the good guy, the sympathetic interrogator. "And Karen? She's an attractive young woman. No one could blame you if—"

"She's a baby!" Larry protested. "What could I possibly have in common with someone like her?"

"You're right," Dallas agreed. "She's way too young. But maybe she saw you with someone else? Maybe she has information that you don't want shared?"

"Are you crazy?" Larry snapped. "She got to town two years ago. What could she possibly know that could hurt me?"

"That's a good question," Stella said. "How about you answer it?"

Chance's phone buzzed, and he saw that Trinity had texted him.

Interesting tidbit. Guess whose father owns an antiques store in town?

He didn't have to ask. He knew.

Everything was clicking into place. All the little clues—the overeager young woman, the antique weapons, the missing antique frame, Beatrice's comment about Karen nosing around in the house.

"What is it?" Stella asked, and he handed her the phone, watching as she read the message.

He knew the moment the truth hit her, saw her eyes narrow, her expression tighten.

"Change of plans," she said, thrusting the phone back. "We're going to town. There's a little antiques shop I'd like to visit."

Larry stiffened, his shoulders suddenly straight, his face even paler. He didn't argue. Didn't try to make them change their mind.

Chance got the address from Trinity, gave it to Dallas, then texted his sister.

Keep Karen out of the room and away from Beatrice. Don't let Beatrice out of your sight. We're going to the antiques shop. Will keep you posted.

He shoved the phone into his pocket and detached the ankle strap he used to carry his extra pistol.

"Just in case," he said, handing it to Stella. She nodded, adjusting the straps so they'd fit her calf, checking the firearm to be sure it was loaded, the safety on. She looked confident, assured, ready.

She also looked heartbroken.

"It's going to be okay," he said.

"You keep telling me that."

"Because I believe it." He squeezed her hand, and her fingers wove through his. They sat just like that as Dallas sped toward town.

TWELVE

Everything was about to change.

Stella felt that to the depth of her soul.

The fact that Larry hadn't said one word, asked one question or protested the change in plans seemed to confirm that.

She wanted to poke at him a little, ask more questions that she knew he wouldn't answer, but he looked terrible—his face ashen, his lips colorless.

She thought he might pass out and, despite the fact that she knew he had something to do with the attacks, despite the fact that she was sure he'd withheld important information, she couldn't stop herself from caring.

"Are you okay, Uncle Larry?" she asked.

When he didn't answer, she leaned over the seat, felt the pulse in his carotid artery. Steady but too fast, his heart beating at an alarming rate.

"You need to calm down, take a couple of deep breaths. Whatever is going on, we'll handle it," she said.

"This is all my fault," he responded so softly she almost didn't hear.

"Whatever *this* is," she responded, "it can be fixed. You just have to tell us what's going on."

"I can't."

"You *won't*," Chance replied, his tone harsh. He'd always put his family first. He'd never have made the choice to keep silent if it would hurt the people he loved.

There was no way he could understand someone like Larry.

Stella couldn't, either, but he was her family, and she wanted to believe there'd been extenuating circumstances, some reason besides money or lust that had driven him to keep secrets that had almost gotten Beatrice and Stella killed.

"I can't," Larry repeated, the words breaking, his hands trembling as he smoothed his hair, tried to pull himself together. "It's a horrible choice. Like trying to decide which child to feed when you only have enough food for one and both are starving, and you know one of them is going to die, and all you can do is hope that you can save the other."

"What are you talking about, old man?" Dallas asked, his hands tight on the steering wheel.

"He said he'd kill Patty. He told me that if I said anything to anyone about who he was, he'd kill her."

"Who?" Chance asked, but Larry was done, his lips pressed together, his jaw tight.

"Better call local law enforcement," Dallas suggested. "We might want backup when we get to the antiques shop."

Stella called Cooper's direct number, gave him as much information as she had as quickly as she could. He promised to meet them at the shop. Old Thymes. That's what it was called. He knew it, had been there on several occasions. He even knew that the owner was Karen's father. Camden Woods was the guy's name. He'd been in town for a couple of years, and Cooper hadn't heard any complaints about him or the business. Maybe that's why he hadn't put the shop and Camden together with the attack. That's what he'd said to Stella, but she could hear the

frustration and irritation in his words. He was frustrated
with himself, annoyed that he hadn't made the connection.

By the time he disconnected, they were in town, the
familiar buildings and pretty streets belying whatever
secret was hiding there. Stella had walked Main Street
hundreds of times. As a kid, she'd hung out on the street
corners, playing tag with friends and eating ice cream
from the local shop.

Despite all the heartache, she'd had a good childhood.

She needed to remember that just as clearly as she remembered the rest.

"Looks like we're here," Dallas said, pulling around
the side of the old brick building that housed the shop. "It
would be good to know what we're walking into, don't you
think?" He shifted so that he was looking straight at Larry.

"I told you, if I talk—"

"Your wife dies. Yeah. We got that part, man," Dallas
said. "But you know what? She's probably going to die
anyway. Along with other people you love. All because
you decided to keep your mouth shut."

Larry blinked, shook his head. "I can't."

"Then the consequences are going to be on your head.
Get out. We're going in that shop, and we're going to have
a little talk with the guy who owns it," Chance said, none
of the usual politeness in his voice.

He was angry.

So was Stella.

She waited until Chance got out of the SUV, then she
followed, the weight of the gun strapped to her ankle
comfortingly familiar. She'd been trained by the navy,
and she'd continue to train in combat and self-defense
since she'd left it. She didn't take things for granted, and
she wasn't content to rest on her laurels.

She hadn't done her due diligence, though.

As angry as she was with her uncle, she was just as

upset with herself. She should have run a background check on Karen, asked for references, talked to some of the people who knew her. Someone somewhere might have known something that would have kept Beatrice safe.

Too late now.

All Stella could do was move forward.

She walked to the front of the shop with Chance, Larry shuffling along behind them. Dallas was there, too, hanging back, flanking them and searching for trouble.

A sign hung from the shop window, the bold letters declaring that the place was closed.

"Odd for a shop in this area of town to be closed during business hours, don't you think?" Chance asked, banging on the door.

"Odder that it looks nearly empty inside." She peered in through the storefront window, eyeing shelves that looked mostly empty. Someone had left a light on in the back room.

As she watched, a shadow moved, blocking the light for a split second.

"There's someone in there," she said.

Chance yanked her away from the window, placing his body between hers and the glass. "Let's not take chances, Stella. A bullet can go through a store window just as easily as it can go through the window of an SUV."

"How many entrances does this building have?" Dallas asked, stepping back and looking at the upper stories. Three of them. All with windows glinting in the sunlight.

"Front and back," Larry said. "And a fire escape in the alley."

"Whoever is in there is going to have to come out," Chance said, moving to the window and peering into the shop. "Light is off, so he or she may be on the way. You want to take the back door, Dallas? Stella and I will watch the fire escape. My guess is that he's going that way."

"Will do," Dallas responded, jogging around the side of the building.

"We should wait for Cooper," Larry suggested, his voice shaking. "Whoever is in there probably isn't the kind of person you should mess with."

Chance laughed, the sound harsh and ugly. "You've got that wrong, Larry. We're not the kind of people *he* should mess with. There's the sheriff's car. I suggest that you stay here and explain things to him."

He took off before Larry could respond.

Stella followed.

As much as she wanted to hear the truth, as much as she wanted to force it out of her uncle, she wanted to help Chance more.

Despite Chance's suggestion, Larry followed along behind them, his breath hitched with fear as they entered the narrow alley.

"This isn't a good idea," he said nervously, beads of sweat on his brow despite the frigid temperature. "He's not a nice guy."

"Who?" Chance asked. "Or are you content to just let whoever it is get away with terrorizing you and your family?"

Larry closed his eyes, swayed. "Camden Woods," he whispered. "My youngest son."

Chance heard the words. He even understood them. He just wasn't sure how it all fit. Now wasn't the time to figure it out. They needed to get in the shop, see if the person moving around in there was Camden.

Larry's son?

If so, he wasn't a son that anyone in the family had known about. That explained a lot, but it didn't explain everything.

Stella looked stunned, but she didn't question her uncle's assertion.

"Go to the front of the shop," she said. "Tell Cooper everything you know. Being honest is the best thing you can do right now. I'm going up the fire escape. If the guy doesn't want to come out on ground level, he'll head to the roof and try to escape to the next building."

She was probably right. Less than four feet wide, the alley was little more than a space between buildings, the ground littered with debris and dusted with snow. The fire escape was near the back corner, the metal rusted and old. If a person were brave enough to try it, they could make it to the roof and jump to the next roof.

Brave enough or desperate enough.

"I've ruined everything, Stella," Larry said. "I didn't mean to. I just never thought that a mistake I made forty-five years ago would come back to haunt me. I panicked, and I made everything worse. I hope you can forgive me. I hope Patty and Beatrice and my kids can."

He looked…lost. Like a man who'd been walking in one direction for a long time and suddenly realized he'd taken the wrong path and had no idea where he was or how to get back.

Stella must have seen that.

She pulled him into a quick hug, then gave him a gentle shove away. "We'll work it out. Now go talk to Cooper."

Larry looked stricken, but he turned and walked away.

"Let's get this done," Stella said, impatience in her voice as she reached the fire escape. Above it, someone had fashioned a bridge between buildings. From Chance's angle, it looked like several two-by-fours side by side.

"Careful," he cautioned as Stella grabbed hold of the rail and put her foot on the first rung of the fire escape. "That thing doesn't look like it will bear weight."

"It should. There's got to be a code, right? Fire safety

inspections? Something that guarantees this thing is functional in case of emergency."

"I wouldn't count on it," he said, yanking at the metal frame. It held firm, but he still didn't trust it.

A soft sound came from somewhere above—wood against wood as a window opened. Third floor. Chance could see someone in the window, climbing over the ledge and onto the metal landing.

Female.

That was his first impression.

Karen. That was his second. Same hair. Same build. Young, moving like she'd done this a dozen times before. She reached back inside, pulled out a large duffel and set it on the landing. Then she levered half her body into the window, dragged what looked like an oversize flowerpot from inside.

She hefted it in both arms, wobbled to the railing.

Looked down.

Chance had about a millisecond to realize what she was going to do. Then the pot was falling, and he was diving toward Stella, tackling her to the ground, twisting so that his body hit the pavement first.

The pot landed a foot away, bits of clay flying into the air, dirt sprinkling Chance's face and arms.

He jumped up, dragging Stella with him.

He brushed the debris from her hair and shoulders. "You okay?"

"Dandy. Now how about we get that little monster? Because I've about had enough of her." She was climbing the first set of fire escape stairs before he could respond.

He followed, the metal vibrating as they raced toward the roof.

Karen had already made it there. Chance could see her, easing out onto the makeshift bridge on her hands and knees, the duffel hanging from her shoulders, bumping against her back as she crawled across the area between the buildings.

Didn't matter.

She wasn't going far.

Dallas was waiting for her, standing on the roof of the other building, just far enough away that Karen probably couldn't see him. Oblivious, she just kept crawling, completely focused on her escape.

Stella reached the roof a second ahead of Chance, and by the time he was up, she'd made it to the bridge. She didn't pull her gun, didn't call out to try to stop Karen. She just watched as the young woman eased across the boards.

"How long do you think it's going to take for her to realize she's been caught?" she asked as he reached her side.

"I'd say about three seconds."

"One," Stella said. "Two."

Karen had reached the other side and was scrambling over the roof ledge. She straightened and looked right at them, smiling triumphantly.

"Sorry about this, Stella. No hard feelings, right?" she called, pushing the boards so that they tumbled down into the alley. "See you around, cousin!"

She turned, saw Dallas and screamed so loudly Chance was certain the foundations of the buildings shook.

She pulled the duffel from her back, tossed it with all her strength. It fell short of Dallas, but she was already running to whatever entrance Dallas had used to gain access to the roof.

Another fire escape?

A door from the building?

"Should I call Cooper and tell him what's going on?" Stella asked.

"Not unless you think Dallas can't handle this."

"He can."

He did. A quick sprint, and Dallas had Karen by the arm, hauling her up against his side.

"Looks like he's got it under control. Let's head back down. Cooper should be there with your uncle, and I'm anxious to hear what he has to say."

"You and me both." She turned away from the drama unfolding on the other roof. Not much of a drama, really. Dallas was nudging Karen toward the opposite side of the building.

She wasn't screaming anymore.

She looked like a kid caught with her hand in the cookie jar, the duffel she'd been trying to escape with now in Dallas's hands. "Wonder what is in the bag?" Chance said more to himself than to Stella.

"I have a feeling some of it came from Beatrice's house."

"Do you think Larry was telling the truth?"

"About Camden being his son?" She shrugged, stepping onto the fire escape and beginning her descent. "Why would he lie?"

"Why wouldn't he have acknowledged Camden two years ago, when he moved to town?"

"Knowing my uncle, he didn't want to hurt Patty. He was probably hoping he could keep the relationship a secret, maybe have some kind of connection with Camden but not one that anyone would be suspicious of."

"Have you ever met the guy?"

"No." She'd reached street level and stood waiting for him, her hair shimmering in the sunlight that shone between the buildings, her cheeks red from exertion or emotion or both.

This couldn't be easy for her, but she was handling it like she did every mission—with focus and determination.

When he reached her side, she smiled, shaking her head. "You're a mess, Chance."

"Thanks?"

She laughed, brushing dirt from his shoulders, then from his hair, her hands lingering a little longer than was necessary. He knew that. She knew it, and that smile was still in place, her gaze direct and unapologetic. "We have a lot to talk about. One day. When we're not dodging bullets or clay pots."

"What is there to say, Stella? We either go for it or we don't. There's never going to be any in-between for us."

Her smile slipped away, and she nodded. Solemnly. Carefully. As if that one gesture spoke every word that needed to be said. "I don't ever want to be hurt again, Chance. I don't ever want to love and then be left alone. The thought of that terrifies me. But you know what terrifies me more?"

"What?"

"The thought of never having that kind of love. The kind that takes up all the empty places in my heart. The kind that would hurt to lose, but that would leave memories that would make the pain worth it. Come on. Let's go find Cooper and Larry. Let's figure out what Karen had in that bag. Let's get this mess cleaned up because Christmas is coming and I promised Beatrice we'd hang the stockings."

He could have said a dozen things to that. He could have given her all sorts of reassurances. She didn't want that, though. He knew Stella. Just like he knew himself.

"Chance? Stella?" Cooper appeared at the end of the alley, Larry beside him. "Everything okay here?"

"One of my men caught Karen Woods trying to escape through the building next door," Chance responded.

"I've got a man over there now."

"I guess my uncle told you what's going on," Stella said, and Cooper nodded.

"Most of it."

"All of it," Larry corrected.

"We'll see if your story checks out, Larry," Cooper responded, and Larry flinched.

"Why would I lie about something like this?"

"Because you're in deeper than you want to admit?" Cooper suggested. "Because maybe you're having financial difficulties and you want your sister's estate to help you get back on your feet. Maybe you hired Camden to make sure you got it?"

"He's been blackmailing me for two years. That's how I got into the financial trouble I'm in."

"Because he's your long-lost son?" Cooper asked.

"I told you he is! Patty had no idea that I'd had an affair, and I never thought…" His voice trailed off and he shook his head.

He hadn't thought he'd get caught?

He hadn't thought he'd have to pay the consequences of his sin?

Chance didn't ask.

He'd seen it too many times. The sin. The results. The sadness that followed.

"Maybe you should have thought," Stella said quietly, and Larry started to cry. Quiet tears that streamed down his face.

"When Camden's mother told me she was pregnant, she asked for ten thousand dollars cash so she could leave town. I gave it to her, because I didn't know what else to do."

"Maybe confess?" Chance suggested.

"I couldn't hurt my wife like that. I thought I could pay the money, and it would all go away, but then Camden showed up and told me that if I didn't pay, he'd go to Patty."

"So you did?" Cooper asked, and Larry nodded.

"What else could I do?"

A lot, but Chance didn't say it.

He could picture the first meeting, could imagine Larry's shock. He'd been living a lie for forty-five years, and now it was all going to unravel.

"I paid until I was out of money, but he kept wanting more," Larry continued. "I told him that, and he told me he'd take care of it."

"He must have known Beatrice didn't have a will," Stella said. "He must have known about your father's stipulation regarding the house and the property."

"He knows everything. More than me. He's fixated on the family." Larry wiped moisture from his cheeks. "If he could get you out of the way, Stella, it was only a matter of time before—"

"Stop," Cooper ordered. "You have rights, Larry. You're well aware of them."

"I gave up my rights when I betrayed my wife and my family."

"I'd still rather you get a lawyer," Cooper said. "I've got a warrant issued for Camden, and I've petitioned for a search warrant of this property and of Camden and Karen's house. They live about a mile from here."

"Has anyone been over there yet?"

"I sent a deputy. No one's home."

"I don't like the sound of that," Stella muttered, meeting Chance's eyes.

He knew what she was thinking.

Exactly what he thought—they needed to get back to the hospital. He pivoted, headed back toward the SUV.

"You don't think he's at the hospital, do you?" She was following him now, running behind him as he sprinted for the vehicle.

"Where's Dallas?" she asked as they reached it. "We need the keys."

"I'll get—" His phone rang, and he saw that it was Trinity.

"Hello?" he said.

"She's gone!" Trinity cried. "You've got to get back here because she's gone!"

"Beatrice?" he asked, and Stella froze, all the blood draining from her face.

"She went for an X-ray. They said an orderly would bring her back out. I waited outside radiology, but she never came back."

"We'll be there as quickly as we can. Contact hospital security."

"Simon is already with them. I can't believe I let this happen. I should have—"

"We'll be there soon."

He disconnected and sprinted back to the front of the store, adrenaline pouring through him because he knew beyond a shadow of a doubt that Camden had Beatrice.

How long had she been missing?

How far could he have gotten?

Cooper would need to put on an APB on whatever vehicle was registered to Camden. He'd have to—

Stella grabbed his arm, yanked him to a stop.

"He has her, doesn't he?" Her eyes were bright with tears, but she didn't let them fall.

"Yes," he said, hating having to say it. "But it's going to be okay," he promised, and he prayed that he was right. Prayed that she wouldn't be disappointed, heartbroken, hurt. Because Beatrice was all she had left of her little family, and he thought it just might destroy Stella to lose her.

She took a shaky breath, nodded stiffly.

"Okay. Let's go find her." Then she took off, sprinting toward Cooper and the deputy.

THIRTEEN

By the time they'd arrived at the hospital, Beatrice had been missing for forty minutes. Not long, but to Stella it seemed like a lifetime. She'd listened while Cooper had questioned the hospital staff; she'd ridden with Chance as they'd headed over to the sheriff's department.

Now she was pacing Cooper's office, waiting while he questioned Karen. Chance and Simon were with him in the interrogation room. They'd left Stella and Trinity together. Stella wasn't sure where Uncle Larry was. All she really cared about was finding Beatrice.

Trinity sat a few feet away, slouched in a chair and crying. "I should have insisted," she said, her eyes red-rimmed from tears. "I should have told them that I had to go with her." She'd said it a dozen times before, and Stella had responded the same way each time.

"It wasn't your fault," Stella assured her, her throat dry with fear. Did Beatrice understand what had happened? Was she afraid? Was she hurt?

The thought left a dull ache in her chest and a twisting pain in her gut. She couldn't just sit around hoping that Beatrice would be found. She had to act.

She walked to the door, yanked it open.

"I'm going to look for her," she said.

"You can't!" Trinity protested.

"Watch me," she replied, stalking down the corridor and pausing outside a closed door.

She could hear voices. Female. Male.

She knocked. Didn't wait for an invitation. Just walked into the room.

They were all there—Chance, Simon, Dallas. Larry. Cooper.

Karen.

For the first time in longer than she could remember, Stella saw red. Her body went cold with rage, her skin crawling with anger.

She walked across the room, ignoring Chance's look of caution.

"You'd better hope that my grandmother is okay," she nearly spat, and Karen frowned.

"My father would never hurt her," she responded blithely, her legs crossed, her fingers tapping impatiently on her thigh. "She's family."

"I'm family, too," Stella responded. "He tried to kill me."

"You're kidding, right? My father barely even knew you existed," Karen scoffed. "I'm sure he was too busy cashing the checks Uncle Larry was writing to bother with you."

"I never wrote him a check," Larry said faintly.

"You gave him cash. Same difference, really." She shrugged. "He's just taking what he's owed. That's all."

"What does he think he's owed?" Chance asked.

"Whatever the rest of the family has." She shrugged again. "It's only fair. At first, he just wanted to get me through college and get his shop going, but once I started working for Beatrice and realized how much money the family has, the plans changed. Things should be split equally in a family like this, and my father deserves his cut."

"Based on what Larry has said, your father got more than his cut," Cooper said. "And he extorted it. Which is a crime and could get him jail time."

"*Extorted?* That's a heavy word, Sheriff." She flipped her hair over her shoulder, studied her nails. "Go ahead, Granddad," she said, "tell him that's not what happened. You were more than willing to help with the shop and with my education."

"It's true. I was happy to help him. At first. Then he kept coming back for more. He thinks I'm a bottomless well that he can keep pulling from."

"You should have told him that you weren't." She frowned. "It's not like he wanted to drive you into bankruptcy."

"Karen, he didn't care if I had nothing. As long as he got what he wanted. He told me that I'd either find a way to pay or he'd take something more valuable than money from me. He threatened to kill my wife." He put his head in his hands, closed his eyes. "I've made a mess of everything."

"No," Chance broke in. "You made mistakes. Camden is making the mess, and Karen is helping him."

"I haven't done anything," she protested.

Chance reached down and opened the duffel that was sitting on the floor beside him, pulling out a beautiful gilt vase that Stella remembered from her childhood. It had a crack down the center now. Probably from being tossed at Dallas.

"Where'd this come from?" he asked, and Karen blushed.

"Beatrice gave it to me."

"Did she give you this, too?" He lifted a gold bracelet decorated with rubies and sapphires.

"I want a lawyer," Karen responded.

"I'll get you one," Cooper said. "Once we book you.

Of course, if you want to tell us where your father has taken Beatrice—"

"He didn't take her anywhere! He wouldn't. I keep telling you—"

"Does your father have an old bowie knife in the shop? One with symbols carved into the handle?" Chance asked.

Karen frowned. "Yes. Why?"

"That's what was used the night Stella was attacked at the hospital."

"My father isn't a murderer," she responded, but her brow furrowed, and she bit her lip.

"You're wondering if he is, kid," Dallas broke in. "So I'd say you have your doubts. How about you try some honesty and either prove your doubts or put them to rest?"

"I've already told you everything I know."

"You haven't told us where you were going with this stuff." Chance nudged the bag with his foot.

"If I tell you, will you agree not to press charges?" She was looking straight into Stella's eyes and, for the first time since she'd met her, Stella saw the resemblance to Larry. The shape of the eyes. The color. They were almost identical.

"That depends on what you know and what you've done," she answered honestly, and Karen blushed.

"I did take a few things. Dad asked me to. He said he just wanted a few family heirlooms to remind him of where he'd really come from. Not the rat-infested house his mother raised him in. You guys were like royalty to us, and Dad said Beatrice would never know anything was missing. He told me that we wouldn't sell anything until after she was gone. We'd just keep them and enjoy them. I let him convince me. I bought the whole we're-family-and-we-deserve-it thing. I knew it was wrong, though. And I'm sorry. I was going to bring everything back before we left town. That's why I was in the shop. I was getting the things I'd stored there."

"You were leaving town?" Stella asked, her heart beating wildly, her mind jumping from thought to thought so rapidly she couldn't quite hold on to any of them.

"Dad said we needed to. He said the guys you had with you were snooping around, and he didn't want to cause any trouble for Larry. He and Derrick—"

"Who's Derrick?" Cooper asked.

"Derrick Smith. He and Dad go way back. They were buddies in the army. When they got out, they both got married and lived right next door to each other. When my mom died, Derrick's wife kind of stepped in and mothered me. She left him a couple of years ago, and he and Dad started thinking up schemes to get money and open their own business. That's how all this started."

"Is Derrick living in town?" Cooper asked, and Karen shook her head.

"No. He lives in Florida. Where we came from. He came up here a few weeks ago for a visit. He's renting a little cabin in the mountains. One of those hunting lodges."

"Have you been there?" Stella asked, all her thoughts suddenly sharply focused. A cabin would be the perfect place for Camden and Derrick to take Beatrice. The perfect place to get what they wanted and discard what they didn't.

And, of course, they wouldn't want Beatrice.

Not once they got what they needed from her.

Bank account information, maybe?

Would she remember that?

What would they do if she didn't?

"I was there once. He doesn't even have hot water or heat. Just a wood stove that he has to keep lit." She wrinkled her nose, brushed a smudge of dirt from her pants. "I was going to meet them there after I returned Beatrice's things."

"Kid," Dallas cut in, his frustration obvious. "You weren't returning anything."

He was right about that. Karen had nearly dropped a flowerpot on Stella's head, and she'd gloated about her victory.

Obviously, she wasn't as innocent as she'd like everyone to think.

But maybe she wasn't as guilty as she looked.

She seemed willing to share some information, and Stella was willing to listen.

"I was, too," Karen protested. "Anyway, we were going to drive from there to Florida. Straight shot. No stops. That's what Dad said. I'd have rather stayed here, but with the shop closed—"

"There's an old hunting lodge twenty minutes west of here," Trinity suddenly said, her gaze on her phone. "Looks like they rent cabins during hunting season."

"That's probably the place," Karen said. "No one is there right now. I can tell you that."

"Your father is," Stella responded, just barely managing to hold in her anger. "Call him. Ask him about Beatrice."

"He doesn't have your grandmother! Besides, if I call him, he'll know something is wrong. He'll hear it in my voice. We're really close, and—"

"Then text him. Ask if Beatrice is okay."

"But—"

"Do it," she demanded. "Because I'm the one who's been most hurt in all of this, and I'm the one who gets to decide whether or not to press charges."

Karen scowled, pulling the phone from her pocket and sending a quick text. Seconds later, her phone buzzed. She glanced at it, her face going white.

"I swear, I didn't know—" she began.

Stella snatched the phone from her hand and read the text.

No worries, hun. The old lady is fine. Go ahead and hang out at the hospital for a while. Don't want anyone getting suspicious, right? Derrick and I have some business to take care of. Meet us at the cabin at midnight. You packed?

"He's got her," she murmured, handing the phone back. The room was buzzing. People talking and planning. That was fine.

They could plan all they wanted.

She was leaving.

She walked out without a word, made it all the way to the end of the hall before Chance caught up with her.

He took her arm. Held it. No pressure, just his fingers wrapped around her bicep.

"Running off without a plan is a good way to get killed," he said quietly.

"She's there. I have to find her."

"My statement still stands."

"You know what they're going to do. Get her financial information. Find out where her accounts are, move the money into their accounts. Then they'll kill her."

"You don't know that."

"Of course I do. They tried to kill me three times because they wanted me out of the way so they could do this. You know that's what it was about. She's vulnerable, and they wanted to take advantage of that. Then I showed up with a bunch of people who weren't going to let that happen, so they kidnapped her. They're going to take what they want and—"

"Stella," he said. Just that, and she stopped talking, looked into his eyes.

Waited, because she knew whatever he said, it was going to be important. This was the Chance she knew best. The one in charge. The one who knew how to run a mission and to save a life.

"Here's how it's going to be," he continued. "I'm sending Trinity back to Beatrice's hospital room. She's going to clean it out and meet us at the house. That's where we're headed. Not to the hunting lodge. Not yet."

"Going to the house will be a waste of time." Stella pulled away, walked out into the cold afternoon. Heavy clouds were moving in from the west, drifting over distant mountains, carrying snow or rain or both. Stella could feel the storm in the air, and all she could think about was Beatrice, in her frilly nightgown, sitting in a freezing cabin with two men who wanted her dead.

"Have I ever led you in the wrong direction?" Chance asked from behind her, and she turned, wanting to rail at him, to yell and scream and demand that he take her straight to Beatrice.

Only he didn't deserve to be treated badly because she was upset. He knew just how scared she was, just how worried she was and just how right *he* was. They needed a plan. Going into a situation like this without one *would* get someone killed.

"What direction do you think we should go?" she asked, forcing a calmness into her voice that she didn't feel.

"We go to your place. We get your car. Give Cooper a chance to get some men together. Then we go to the hunting lodge as a team."

"Chance, what if we're too late?" she asked. "What if they…hurt her before we arrive?"

"It's more likely that they'll keep her alive. At least until they have what they want."

"Okay," she conceded. "We'll do things your way, but I'm going to the hunting lodge as part of the team."

He nodded, motioning for Dallas to get their ride.

She waited impatiently, every beat of her heart reminding her that time was slipping away and, with it, their chances of bringing Beatrice home. She knew how these things worked. She'd recovered hostages in dozens of countries, helped them out of more than a few desperate situations. She'd also failed to bring them out. Not often, but sometimes. Enough that she always worked harder, planned better, prepared more for every mission that she went on.

Time was the enemy.

That was the hard and fast rule of hostage rescue.

The longer the kidnapper had his victim, the less likely it was that the victim would be returned.

She shivered, felt Chance's coat settle around her shoulders. He didn't offer any words of comfort. He didn't tell her that everything would be just fine.

He knew the truth, and as he helped her into Dallas's SUV he whispered in her ear, "God is in control, Stella. Don't forget that."

She nodded, the hard knot of fear still in her stomach.

God was in control.

She knew that.

She just didn't know what He wanted from this.

She didn't know what He'd leave her with when it was over.

Lord, please keep Beatrice safe. And whatever happens, she prayed, *help me make something good out of it.*

It's what her grandfather would have wanted. It's what Beatrice would have wanted.

All *she* wanted was to bring Beatrice home.

After that, she could think about other things. Like the future. Like God's plan. Like Chance, waiting for her to say that she was willing to risk being hurt to love him.

* * *

Chance had worked with plenty of local law enforcement officers. He'd been impressed by most of them, irritated by a few and downright uncivil to any who tried to get in the way of a mission.

Cooper fell into the first category.

He was smart, quick and willing to work as a team. That made things easier, but it still didn't make them good.

Chance eyed the map that had been spread out on Beatrice's kitchen table. Twelve men and women stood around it, taking notes and listening as Cooper outlined the plan.

It was simple enough. They'd park their vehicles at the end of the three-mile gravel road that led to the hunting lodge. Walk in from there. Once they found the cabin, they'd signal the group, and the real fun would begin. They'd take position outside the cabin and wait for Stella to arrive. She'd be driving Karen's car, carrying Karen's cell phone, doing all the things Karen would be doing if she were actually going to meet her father.

Dressed in a winter coat and hood, a scarf over the lower part of her face, Stella would be able to get to the front door without alarming the men.

Once there, she'd knock and walk in like she belonged there, leaving the door wide open for Chance, Dallas and Simon to enter.

Simple.

Easy, even.

Only they had no idea what weapons the two men might have. They had no idea where Beatrice was being kept. Basically, Stella would be walking in blind.

That bothered Chance. A lot.

"We need to rethink the plan," he said, and Cooper frowned.

"Why?"

"Sending Stella in alone is too risky."

"She's not going to be alone. She's going to have nearly a dozen people outside, ready to run to her rescue."

"Not good enough."

"It's plenty good enough," Stella said.

"It won't be if you're dead," he retorted, his blunt words doing absolutely nothing to change Stella's mind.

She grabbed the coat, hat and gloves that one of the deputies had brought from the station. Karen had willingly lent them to the mission. She'd also handed over her cell phone and the keys to her car.

That should have made Chance happy.

It would have, if Stella hadn't been the one going in.

"Why would you think she's going to die?" Dallas asked, leaning against the doorjamb that separated the kitchen from the dining room. "We've been on way more dangerous missions than this one, and we've all come out of them alive."

"This is personal. Emotions are involved. Emotions can get people killed."

"So can standing around discussing things that aren't up for discussion." Stella had strapped on her shoulder holster, and she slid her Glock into place. She still had his ankle holster, and he was pretty certain she had a stun gun hidden in one of the coat pockets. "The sun is going down. By the time we reach the lodge, it will be dark. We've already wasted enough time. Let's head out."

"You cool with that?" Cooper asked, meeting Chance's eyes.

He nodded because Stella was right.

The plan wasn't up for discussion. They'd hashed it out, made decisions and agreed as a team that this was the best way, the *only* way, to get to Beatrice.

No second-guessing.

No backing out.

That had always been his policy. The team knew it.

Cooper gave the signal and his deputies walked out. Dallas and Simon followed.

"You going to stand there all night looking dejected?" Stella asked, pulling on the cap that Karen had lent. Her red hair peeked out from under it, bright against the light blue knit.

"Only if you walk out looking like that."

"What's wrong with the way I look?" She grabbed the duffel that Karen had been carrying. Empty now except for some old books that Stella had tossed in to make it look heavy.

"They get one look at your hair, and it's going to be all over," he murmured, tucking the strands under the knit cap and pulling the hood up over her head. "There. That's better."

"Thanks," she said, and he realized how close they were, how beautiful she looked, standing there in her borrowed snow gear. How big a hole would be left in his life if she were suddenly gone.

"Thank me by staying safe."

"So that we can get through the wretched Christmas season together?" she asked, making light of the situation. She always cracked a joke when they were heading out on a mission, and it always made him smile.

"No, Scrooge," he responded, brushing her lips with his. "You get yourself killed, and all Beatrice's plans for a Christmas engagement will be out the window. She and I will both be devastated."

The words popped out. Unexpected. Right.

He didn't regret them, and she didn't argue with them.

A surprise, because she'd always been the one to back away, deny what they felt.

"Scrooge?" she said. "I guess I've earned my reputation. We'll see if we can fix that when I get back."

He wanted to ask her what she meant, but she was already moving, hefting the duffel onto her shoulder, tossing a scarf around her neck and patting Chance's shoulder like she had a thousand times before. "Let's head out, boss. I've got a grandmother to save."

Outside, snow was beginning to fall, the heavy flakes dancing in the headlights of the three vehicles that sat at the ready.

Stella walked to Karen's small SUV, tossed the bag into the passenger seat and then turned to face him again.

She touched his cheek, her palm warm against his cool skin.

"Just so you know, I'll be careful. I want to come back. For Nana. And for you."

She got into the car, closed the door and turned on the engine.

That was his cue to get moving.

He and his team were leading the caravan.

Twenty miles on snowy roads could take an hour, and they didn't have that much time. Eventually, Woods and Smith would get impatient with Beatrice. They'd get tired of whatever game they were playing. Once they did, anything could happen.

He climbed into Dallas's vehicle, ignoring the worry in the back of his mind. Stella was one of the best operatives he'd ever known. She could handle this, and he had to let her.

"Let's go," he said, and the vehicle jumped forward, bouncing along the long driveway and out onto the snow-dusted road.

FOURTEEN

Stella had been in a lot of dangerous situations. She'd faced a lot of enemies who were much deadlier than Camden Woods or his buddy Derrick Smith. Cooper had provided her with photos of both, and she knew that Derrick had been the one who'd come after her at the hospital. Camden was shorter, stockier and more muscular. She thought that he'd been out in the woods with her, but she couldn't be sure.

Both were former army, but they'd been out of the military for over a decade, and Stella didn't think either had done anything to maintain self-defense or fitness training.

Yeah. She'd faced worse. Military leaders in foreign countries. Hired hit men. Cult leaders who spent every minute of every day getting ready for the Armageddon they were trying to usher in. Camden and Derrick were no danger at all compared to that.

And yet, she was more terrified of them than she'd ever been of anyone. Because they had Beatrice.

She sat in Karen's car, snow falling outside the windows, the night still and quiet around her. She could see the shadows of the police cruisers parked in front of her. They were empty. Just like Dallas's vehicle. The team had headed out thirty minutes ago, and she'd been sitting ever since in the idling car.

Waiting.

Worrying.

Put it in God's hands, and it'll never get dropped, she could almost hear Henry's voice whispering through the darkness.

"Easier said than done," she said out loud, and she knew that if Henry had been around, he'd have laughed.

He'd put everything in God's hands, and he'd never been sorry about it. He'd raised his only son to do the same. Like Henry, Stella's father had been a pastor. She could remember sitting in the wood pew at the front of the church, coloring pictures while he preached.

She'd gotten out of the practice of attending church in recent years. She'd let herself slide away from the old habits that she'd formed as a child. Since she'd returned to Boonsboro, Sunday morning had been for worship again, and she'd found something comforting in that. Seasons changed. People changed. Circumstances and feelings and dreams changed.

But God?

He stayed the same.

Put it in God's hands.

Maybe it wasn't just a pretty little saying designed to make confused and hurting people feel better. Maybe it was something to be done daily: setting all the problems and worries and heartaches in the palms of the one who'd carried every burden, felt every tear.

She really needed to do that.

Now.

Tomorrow.

The day after that.

It's in Your hands, she prayed, closing her eyes, listening to the soft silence that answered.

She used Karen's cell phone and sent Camden a text

saying that she'd gotten tired of sitting around the hospital, and she was on the way.

A few minutes later, the phone buzzed a response. She glanced at it.

See you in a minute, kid.

Good. He was waiting, and she was coming.

It was time to do what she'd been trained for.

She checked her hat and hair in the visor mirror. No stray strands hanging out, announcing her true identity. From a distance, at least, she could pass for just about anyone of a similar height and weight. She grabbed the scarf, wrapped it around her nose and mouth. She was as covered up as she could get, as disguised as possible.

She waited another few minutes, letting the time tick away because she didn't want to arrive too soon. Let Camden and Derrick assume they were home free. Let them get complacent and lazy and careless because all of those things would make it easier to free Beatrice.

If she was in a position to be freed.

The *if* was the part that had been haunting her, the word flitting through her mind over and over again as she waited.

What if...

Beatrice was hurt?

Beatrice was sick?

Beatrice was...worse?

She glanced at the dashboard clock, then texted Chance. Moving in. She put the car in gear and turned onto the gravel driveway that led to the lodge.

She crept along the three-mile stretch, trees brushing the sides of the SUV. The road opened into a clearing, a long building standing in the center of it. The headlights glinted off windows and reflected on the snow that lay on the ground. Karen's cell phone buzzed again and she glanced at it. Bring beer.

Nice thing to ask your daughter to bring to a kidnapping event.

She tucked the phone away. Not bothering to respond.

Karen had mentioned a fork in the road when she'd given directions to the cabin. Stella looked for it, scanning the road, the trees, the tiny little paths that seemed to wind through the forest. When she finally found the forked road, she rolled forward, easing the SUV onto an even narrower stretch of gravel.

Seconds later, she saw a light flashing through the trees. Her pulse jumped, her muscles tense with anticipation. This was it. Everything came down to this one moment.

She thought she saw movement to her left as she climbed out of the car, a shadow shifting at the periphery of her vision. Chance or one of the men moving closer, ready to walk through the door that she was going to leave open.

She stepped onto the porch stairs, and the front door flew open, the man standing in the doorway was the guy from the hospital. She recognized the narrow, wiry build. The height.

Derrick.

She would have said his name, greeted him like an old friend would, but she didn't want her voice to tip him off.

"Didn't you get your dad's text?" Derrick demanded. "We need some more beer here. That old lady is driving us batty. Go on back to town and get some. Buy some food, too, and don't come back until you do."

He slammed the door, and she thought she heard a bolt slide home.

She tried the knob anyway. Locked.

She could see in the front windows, the living room

light making every detail of the room visible. Wide-planked flooring, rough with age and neglect. Easy chair. Saggy couch and beat-up coffee table.

Derrick must have seen her looking. He knocked on the window, motioned for her to go.

"Hurry up. We've got plans for later tonight. Maybe when you come back, you can convince the old lady to cooperate."

He stalked to an easy chair, dropped into it, scowling as he stared Stella down. He didn't seem to know she was an imposter, and she wanted to keep it that way, so she turned her back to the window, hurried down the porch stairs.

No way was she going to give up.

Derrick had mentioned Beatrice. Obviously she was alive and okay.

Stella was going to make sure she stayed that way.

She rounded the small cabin, checking two windows on the side of the small building. Both were locked. She moved around to the back. There was a small deck there, light from a single window illuminating the weathered wood.

She approached it cautiously, easing up the deck steps and peering into a tiny kitchen. Not much in it but a stove and a miniature fridge. A table stood against one wall. A chair. Beatrice was sitting in another chair, her frilly nightgown splattered with dirt, and what looked like a laptop was sitting on the table in front of her.

Were they trying to get her bank account password?

Stella reached for the window, her hand falling away as Camden Woods stepped into view. He walked to the table, jabbed at the computer screen and yelled something that Stella couldn't hear through the glass.

Beatrice seemed unfazed, her shrug only adding to Camden's fury. He stomped away, came back a second later with a pencil and paper. He thrust both into Beatrice's hands and left.

Out to the living room maybe.

Stella didn't waste time. She tried the window. Locked just like the other ones. There was the back door, though, and she fished in her pocket for the utility tool she'd brought.

Chance wasn't the only one who knew how to pick a lock.

She worked quietly, the snow still falling, the night eerily silent. No animals moving through the trees. No night creatures calling out to each other.

The peace of the forest had been disturbed by humans. She could feel their presence, the weight of the eyes that were watching as she fiddled with the lock.

Was everyone in place? Were they ready to move in?

The lock clicked, and she took a deep breath, pressing her ear against the wood, listening. No more yelling. No voices.

She turned the knob, pulling the stun gun from her pocket. Not her weapon of choice but better than using a gun when Beatrice was in the line of fire. She pushed against the door and it creaked open, the sound breaking the silence, breaking the calm.

A man yelled something from the front of the cabin, and footsteps pounded on the floor.

She knew who was coming, and she was prepared, jabbing the stun gun into Derrick's side as he raced toward her. He dropped like lead, falling to the ground with a loud thud.

Camden hadn't appeared, and Stella darted forward, grabbing Beatrice's hand and pulling her to her feet.

"Come on, Nana. We've got to hurry."

The door was still open, and they were so close to escaping. She thought she heard footsteps pounding up the deck stairs, thought she saw a shadow darting toward the door. Chance?

Someone ran through the room in front of her, slamming the door shut before she and Beatrice could reach it. Camden was there, an old-fashioned derringer in hand.

"You just keep getting in my way, don't you?" he shouted, lifting the derringer.

She knew. Saw it in his eyes.

He was going to pull the trigger. She shoved Beatrice away, diving toward him, her hand on his wrist as he fired.

The report rocked them both, the bullet slicing a path through Stella's upper arm. She fell sideways, her hand still on Camden's wrist. Her shoulder hit the wall. Her head followed. She saw stars, but she didn't release her grip.

Beatrice screamed, the sound mixing with the ringing in Stella's ears, the wild pounding of her heart. Something else was pounding. She didn't know what. Couldn't concentrate on anything but gaining control of the gun.

She yanked Camden's arm sideways, twisting his forearm until he dropped the gun. She reached for it, would have had it in her hands, but Derrick was up, groggy but moving. He kicked the gun away, snatched Stella up by the front of her shirt.

"I don't like being messed with," he spat.

"Neither do I." She drove her fist into his throat, heard him gag as he fell back.

She swayed, saw the blood dripping from her left arm, pooling on the wood floor. She needed to stop Camden now. Ten minutes from now, she might not be able to. She took her gun from its holster, raised it.

"Don't," Camden said, his voice deadly calm, and she realized he had the derringer in his hand, the barrel pressed against Beatrice's temple. "You even breathe funny, and I'll kill her."

"If you kill me, you'll never get my bank account information," Beatrice said, her voice shaking.

"It's a little late for that, Granny," Derrick snapped, moving past Stella, his gaze never leaving her face. "Your granddaughter has just cost you everything."

He was afraid.

She could see it in his eyes.

"You cost yourself everything. Greed does that to people. It makes them stupid," she said.

"Shut up. Both of you!" Camden barked, the derringer wavering, his attention jumping to the small window. Had he seen something there?

Stella didn't look, but she felt it—the energy humming in the air, the feeling that something big was about to happen.

"Put your gun on the ground," Camden demanded, easing through a narrow doorway that must have led to the living area. "Any sudden movements and Beatrice dies," he warned.

She could have taken the shot, but she was bleeding heavily and dizzy from it.

She didn't want to miss. Didn't want to hit Beatrice. She set her Glock on the floor.

"That's better." Camden nodded, the derringer dropping a little more, the barrel no longer against Beatrice's head. "We're going out the front door. You follow, she dies. You call the police, she dies. You cooperate, and you might get a few more years with her."

"Right. So don't try anything funny," Derrick said.

As he reached for the Glock, all the energy Stella had been feeling suddenly exploded.

The window shattered, and Derrick fell back, blood staining his shoulder and chest.

Stella was already moving, pulling Chance's gun from the ankle holster, aiming for Camden. He had the derringer up again, pressed against Beatrice's cheek, his arm around her waist.

"Nobody move," he said, and the world seemed to stop. The back door was open, and Dallas and Simon were there, guns drawn, expressions grim.

"I just want to leave here," Camden continued conversationally. "I don't want trouble. I don't want to hurt anyone."

"Then let the lady go," Simon suggested. "And walk right on outside."

"Into whatever trap is waiting for me? I don't think so." He backed up, the gun held against the side of Beatrice's face. She didn't flinch, but Stella could see the whiteness of her skin where the barrel pressed into flesh.

"You're only digging yourself deeper into a hole," Stella said, and she was surprised to hear the thickness of her words. She felt light-headed and woozy, blood still dripping down her fingers. "If you let her go now, you won't face as many charges."

"In for a penny. In for a pound. That's one of the only things my mother ever taught me." Camden's harsh laughter echoed through the room. "Put your weapons down. All of you. If you don't, I will kill Beatrice. I promise you that."

"You really think you're going to make it out of this cabin alive?" Dallas said, taking a step forward, setting his gun on the kitchen table.

Camden still had the derringer, he still had Beatrice and, for the moment, he was still the one in control.

He wouldn't be for long.

Stella knew that.

She trusted that.

Chance was somewhere, and when he showed up, the odds would flip in their favor.

"I said put the weapons down," Camden growled, and

Simon finally complied, setting his Glock on the counter as Stella put her weapon on the floor.

"Good. Now where'd your other buddy go?" Camden asked, backing away, his gaze darting from one person to another, trying to track everyone's movements as he eased into the living room.

Stella followed him.

Cold air swept in from the open front door, the frigid breeze hitting her square in the face.

Camden must have felt the cold, too.

He whirled toward the open door, his grip on Beatrice loosening. That was all Stella needed. She tackled him from behind, rolled with him as they landed on the ground. And then he was over her, the gun under her chin, his eyes blazing.

"You should have stayed away," he panted. "You should never have tried to take what belonged to me!"

She expected to feel the bullet ripping through her flesh, feel her life slipping away.

Instead, she felt the weight of Camden's body as he fell on top of her, heard the clatter of the derringer as it dropped to the floor. Felt warm blood sliding down her neck.

Camden's?

Hers?

She tried to shove him away, but her arms were weak, her muscles unresponsive. She felt groggy and a little confused. Not quite sure what had happened. Camden's body had forced the air from her lungs, and she couldn't catch her breath. Couldn't move him.

And then he was gone.

Pulled away by someone.

By Chance.

He was leaning over her, his brow creased with concern, his hand shaking as he brushed hair from her forehead. "It's okay," he said.

"Then why do you look like it's not?" she managed to say.

"Because you're bleeding like a stuck pig, that's why." He slid out of his jacket, pressed it against the wound in her upper arm.

"Where's Beatrice?"

"Simon brought her outside."

"Is she okay?"

"I didn't see any injuries."

"She needs a coat." She shoved at his hand, trying to push him away so that she could stand. "I've got to find one for her."

"I told Simon to bring her back to the hospital."

"I thought you said she wasn't injured."

"She's still sick, remember," he said gently, and she could see the fear in his eyes. Fear for her.

"I need to see her." She sat up and then realized what a mistake that was. Her head spun, darkness edging in until everything was gone, and it was just her, lying against a warm chest, someone whispering in her ear.

"If you die on me, I'm going to kill you, Stella."

She would have laughed if she could have, would have opened her eyes and told Chance exactly what she thought of him—that he was the best thing that had happened to her in a very long time and that she wasn't sure why it had taken her so long to realize it.

That she loved him, with everything she had. That she was his.

Only her eyes wouldn't open. The words wouldn't come, and she felt herself drifting as voices filled the cabin and the darkness swept her away.

FIFTEEN

One man dead.

Another man wounded.

Stella wounded.

It wasn't the outcome that Chance had been hoping for, but it was better than the alternative: Beatrice dead, Stella dead, more hearts broken, more families lost.

His family lost.

That's what it would have felt like because Stella was a part of him. He'd known that for years, but he'd finally accepted what it meant. Not just teamwork. Not just trust or respect or affection. A deep-seated connection that nothing could ever break.

He pressed his jacket against Stella's arm, his grip tight. He didn't like her pallor, the amount of blood that she'd lost, the fact that she'd slipped into unconsciousness.

His phone buzzed, and he knew it was Trinity asking for an update. Simon would fill her in. He was on the way back to the hospital with Beatrice, and he'd said he would contact Trinity and tell her to meet him there. Dallas was a few feet away, being interviewed by a couple of deputies. He'd fired the shot that had taken Derrick down, and that had provided the distraction that had gotten Chance in the front door.

That had been the plan, and it had gone off almost flawlessly.

Almost.

He scowled, eyeing the blood that splattered the floor beneath Stella's arm.

"You'd better get through this," he muttered.

She didn't respond. Just lay still and pale and silent.

That worried him.

A lot.

Because Stella was always moving, always ready, always fighting.

He kept his jacket pressed to her arm as rescue personnel swarmed the cabin, checking pulses, triaging wounds. Two EMTs were crouching beside Camden, calling information into their radios.

He could have told them not to bother.

The bullet he'd fired had gone straight through Camden's head. Not something Chance was proud of. Taking a life was never the right thing, it was never the easy thing, but sometimes it was the *only* thing.

If he hadn't acted, Stella would be dead.

There'd been no doubt about that. Camden's finger had been on the trigger, and he'd been ready to fire.

A split second to act.

That was all that Chance had, and he'd taken the shot, firing the way he'd been trained—accurately, without hesitation.

"What do we have here?" A young EMT knelt beside him, gauze pads in his hand, gloves on. "Mind if I take a look?"

Chance released the pressure, peeled back his jacket so the guy could poke at the wounds. It looked like the bullet had gone right through Stella's upper arm.

"She'll need to get this cleaned and dressed. Have an X-ray to see if the bullet hit the bone." The guy pressed gauze pads to the entrance and exit wounds, wrapped them tightly.

"Let's start an IV," he called, and another EMT rushed over.

Chance waited impatiently while the IV was started, watching as blood seeped through the gauze. He wanted to nudge the EMTs away, take care of things himself. He'd run IVs before. Stella was the one who'd taught him how. She probably wouldn't be happy if he practiced on her, though. She'd told him he was the worst student she'd ever had. The memory would have made him smile if the situation hadn't been so serious, if she hadn't been just as still and silent as when he was holding the jacket to her wound.

"How bad is it?" Cooper appeared at his side, his gaze shifting from the bloody gauze to the blood on the floor and then to Chance's face.

"Not as bad as it could be. Not as good as I'd like."

"Camden didn't fair so well," Cooper responded, gesturing to the sheet-covered body lying a few feet away.

"It was Stella or him, and it wasn't going to be Stella."

"I know. I saw the whole thing. We'll fill out the paperwork, but I can tell you for sure that no charges will be filed."

"You want my gun until that's official?"

"Yeah. Protocol. You'll have it back once you're cleared."

Chance handed him the Glock.

"Thanks." Cooper frowned. "It's amazing what greed will do to a person. All Camden had to do was accept what Larry was willing to give and none of this would have happened."

"None of this would have happened if Larry had been honest with his wife from the beginning."

"Fear and greed, and now a mess to clean up and a man who could have been anything lying dead on the ground.

It's a shame and a tragedy. Makes me wonder why I do the job I do."

"To keep this from happening more often?" Chance offered, knowing how much it hurt to see the worst of life, to always view the world through lenses tainted from seeing atrocities, the most heinous of crimes. He fought that every day, worked hard to find the good in the midst of the tragedies. It was tough, though, and obviously Cooper was feeling that.

"I guess you're right about that." He sighed, rubbed the back of his neck. "I'll have to drive out and tell Karen that her father is gone."

"That's hard news to give."

"Hard news to hear, too. She was a pawn in a game she didn't know was being played."

She also committed several crimes for her father.

Maybe she'd learned her lesson. Maybe she hadn't. That wasn't up to Chance to decide.

Camden's army buddy, on the other hand, needed to go away for a long, *long* time.

"How's Smith doing?" he asked. "From what I saw he survived the bullet."

"Looked worse than it was. It glanced off his collarbone. Lots of blood, but he's still alive. Cursing up a storm and threatening all kinds of consequences."

"Like?"

"Guess he thinks he can sue your organization and the Boonsboro Sheriff's Department. He'll be thinking differently once we book him and read him the list of charges."

"Does he know Camden is dead?"

"I told him. That's why he's making threats. Like I said, he'll shut up once he realizes how much trouble he's in. I'm going to ride in the ambulance with him. He's got a lot of questions to answer and a lot of crimes to answer for. I'm bringing the state police in, asking them to process and collect evidence. I don't want the guy to get off on a technicality."

"That's a good call."

"For the record, your team did good. You planning to stick around here? Or are you going to the hospital? I'm going to need to take your statement later. I can do it there or at the station."

"I'll be at the hospital," he responded.

"I'll call you when I'm finished with Smith. We can figure out a place to talk then. When Stella comes to, tell her I'm sorry things went down this way. I was hoping we'd get through this without any casualties."

"I'm not out," Stella murmured. "So I won't be coming to."

She opened her eyes, glanced at the IV the EMT was adjusting. She was pale as paper—her cheeks and lips devoid of color.

"And things happen, right?" she continued. "We can't know every variable, and we can't plan for them all. So what's to apologize for?"

"The fact that you were shot, maybe?" Cooper said.

"I've had way worse than this."

Chance smiled. *This* was the Stella he knew.

"Okay. No apology then, but how about the next time Beatrice needs to be saved it's from somewhere like a flower garden or a grassy meadow. No snow, no guys with guns, no chance for anyone to be hurt."

Stella chuckled, then groaned. "Save the jokes for when my arm isn't about to fall off. I'll be able to appreciate them better."

"You got it, kid." Cooper unloaded Chance's Glock, dropped the gun and the cartridge into an evidence bag. "The ambulance is getting ready to transport Smith. I'm heading out. You need anything before our meeting, let me know."

He walked away, and Stella reached for Chance's hand, her palm cold and dry against his. "You weren't lying to me, were you?"

"About what?"

"Beatrice. She's okay, right?"

"She seemed to be," he answered carefully.

"What aren't you telling me?" she demanded, and he couldn't lie to her.

"She was upset. Her breathing was a little rough. Simon is on the way to the hospital with her. Trinity is going to meet them there."

"Rough how?"

"I was a little distracted by the amount of blood you were losing to qualify the sound," he said dryly.

If she noticed his tone, she didn't let on.

"I need to find out if the X-rays were done."

"They were. The nurse had just wheeled Beatrice out of X-ray and handed her over to the orderly when she was taken."

"The orderly was Derrick or Camden?" she asked.

"Probably. Cooper is looking into it."

"I'm glad the X-ray was done. I need to see if they're going to put her on antibiotics. If she has pneumonia, she's going to need a stronger treatment protocol." She tried to sit up, and he pressed his hand to her shoulder, looked her straight in the eye.

"Don't."

"Don't what?"

"Try to stand."

"I don't see why I shouldn't."

"Because you're in no shape to, ma'am," the EMT answered. He motioned for two of his coworkers who were standing by with a gurney. "You've lost too much blood. You try to stand up, and you're going to fall over."

Stella frowned. "You don't really think I'm going to let

you roll me out on that gurney, do you? Because there's no way—"

Chance scooped her up before she could protest, set her on the gurney and leaned down so that they were eye to eye. He could see the golden tips of her red lashes, the tiny flecks of gold in her blue eyes. He could see the fine lines that fanned out from the corners of them, and the little scar at the edge of her brow.

He could see *her*, every bit of who she was—stubborn and strong and determined to be there for the people she loved.

"You want to check on Beatrice, right?" he asked.

"Yes, but—"

"This is the quickest way to get there."

She frowned, but there was a glint of humor in her eyes. "You're clever, Chance. I'll give you that."

"I'm also worried. Do me a favor and don't make that worse by refusing to cooperate with treatment protocol."

She touched his cheek, shook her head. "You don't have to worry about me, Chance. I'm going to be fine. What choice do I have? Beatrice needs me."

"I need you, too, Stella," he admitted. "So how about we make sure you're as okay as you say you are?"

"You don't need me, Chance. You're the most independent, confident, accomplished person I know. The only thing you need is to loosen up a little, maybe wear those flannel shirts more often. Ditch the tie. Have a little—"

He kissed her softly. Gently. Felt all the words die on her lips and the tension ease from her muscles, and he knew that everything they could be together was right there in that moment—supportive, connected, loved.

"What was that for?" she asked, and he brushed the bangs from her forehead, kissing the silky skin beneath it.

"Just practicing."

"For?"

"Mistletoe moments," he responded, and she smiled.

"You're assuming there will be mistletoe."

"I'm not assuming. I'm planning."

She laughed at that, taking his hand and holding on tight as the EMT wheeled her out into the falling snow.

EPILOGUE

Christmas had exploded all over the house.

Every nook and cranny was filled with it. Little trees. Big ones. Stockings and tinsel and lights. There were garlands on the banister and wrapped around the porch pillars. Pretty little pinecones, hand-painted with glitter, sat in a basket on the fireplace mantel right next to the photo of Henry and Beatrice that had been found with a cache of antiques in the trunk of Camden's car. Someone had put a red bow on the corner of the frame and sat a porcelain angel next to it.

Yep. Christmas. Everywhere.

The old Stella would have hated it, would have wanted to avoid it like the plague.

The new Stella?

She was enthralled, amazed by the stunning beauty of it all.

She stood in the parlor, looking at the tree she and Chance had helped Beatrice choose and thinking about how lovely it was. A blue spruce, its silvery needles the perfect backdrop for all the ornaments Beatrice and Trinity had hung on it.

Karen had helped, too, but she'd been more somber than the other two, her sadness at losing her father, her disappointment in the choices he'd made, only partially hidden. She'd been given community service and three years probation. She'd also had to return every item she'd taken from Beatrice.

She was facing it all with aplomb.

She knew she'd been wrong.

She knew her situation could be worse.

But she sure wasn't trying to be cheerful about things.

A real downer was what Trinity had whispered in Stella's ear.

It was true, but Karen was family. She had no money and nowhere to go, and Stella hadn't had the heart to send her away. She'd offered a room on the condition that she complete the community service work and go to weekly counseling appointments.

Karen had agreed to the terms. She spent two hours at the community center every week, working with at-risk youth. She worked hard, and was keeping up with her schoolwork and her volunteer work at the hospital. Stella had high hopes that she'd get through the tragedy and become someone better because of it.

Larry and Patty were discussing taking her in and allowing her to stay until her graduation, but the two needed some time to work through Larry's betrayal and his lies.

To her credit, Aunt Patty had been gracious.

She hadn't kicked him out of the house, hadn't demanded a divorce and hadn't told him that what he'd done was unforgivable. She was angry, though, and she'd been more than happy to tell Stella just how heartbroken she felt.

Stella had watched her aunt cry. She'd hugged her. She'd promised that she'd stand beside her. No matter what she decided. In the end, Patty had decided that her marriage was worth fighting for.

One mistake in forty-five years. A big one, but I still love him, and I can't throw away all the good because of something that happened decades ago. That's what she'd said to Stella when she'd asked for help finding a good marriage counselor.

Stella had put out feelers, had gotten her aunt and uncle set up with twice-weekly counseling sessions.

Tonight, Larry and Patty would be at church with their entire family. It was Christmas Eve, and they planned to celebrate that together.

Stella was celebrating, too.

The season. The joy of renewal and hope.

Love.

She smiled, running her hand down the pretty dress Trinity had helped her pick out. Her arm was still in a cast, the cracked bone knitting itself back together, but she'd still managed to shimmy into the outfit, make her hair look presentable and put on a little makeup.

Trinity had approved.

Trinity had come to stay for a while. Supposedly to help Stella while she healed, but Stella thought it had more to do with Beatrice. The two had bonded over *Little Women* and Christmas decorations. Tomorrow, Trinity would make the drive to DC to spend Christmas with her family.

Tonight?

She was in Boonsboro, helping Beatrice get ready for Christmas Eve service.

The doorbell rang, the sound of it making a dozen butterflies take flight in Stella's stomach.

Chance.

He'd had work in DC for the past couple of days, but he'd promised to attend Christmas Eve service with her.

He never broke a promise. She'd always known that about him.

Now she knew even more.

She knew all the little things that made him special.

That he loved to walk through the snowy woods.

That he preferred marshmallows in his hot chocolate.

That he loved her and he always would.

She rushed to the door and opened it, and then she was in his arms, the warmth of his embrace filling her heart with joy.

"You made it," she murmured against his lips.

"I wouldn't have missed it for the world," he responded.

"The world is full of wonderful things," she said, her good arm wrapped around his waist.

"Not as wonderful as Christmas with you," he responded, and she laughed.

"Is your family upset that you and Trinity aren't spending Christmas Eve with them?"

"Actually," he said, "they aren't because I invited them here."

She pulled back, looked into his eyes. "Are you kidding?"

"Do I look like I am?"

"Chance…" She didn't even know what to say because she'd been thinking about his family, about how hard it would be for them to have two members gone on a holiday that they always tried to spend together. She'd felt guilty for that, but Beatrice had fought two bouts of pneumonia, and she couldn't travel. Stella had tried to convince Chance not to come, but he'd wanted to be there, and she'd wanted him to be, and all of her protests had been weak and a little ambivalent.

So, yes, she'd been thinking about his family, worrying about them. But she hadn't expected them to show up on her doorstep.

She was ready to commit to Chance.

She was ready to move forward with him.

She wasn't sure she was ready to meet his folks.

She smoothed her hand down her dress, eyed the closed door.

"Are they outside?" she asked, wondering if a dozen Millers were pressed against the wood, waiting to enter.

"Yes. We drove here together. I ran it by Beatrice and she approved. Didn't you notice Trinity and Karen cleaning the guest rooms?"

"I thought they'd gone on a Christmas decorating frenzy. I had no idea they were getting ready for company. Are your parents here, too? Or just your siblings and their kids?"

"They're here," he confirmed, and she suddenly felt a little sick and a little excited and a whole lot unsure.

"You should have told me—" she began, but he shook his head and smiled.

"Beatrice and I decided that it would be best to keep you in the dark. She didn't want you to be nervous."

"Nervous? I'm… I don't know if I'm ready."

"For making new memories?" he asked, tucking a strand of hair behind her ear, kissing her again, that one sweet touch of his lips chasing away her anxiety. "Because that's all this is, Stella. A chance to fill all the darkness with light. To see all the beautiful things that have come out of the difficulties."

"It's also an opportunity for me to look like a total idiot. I should have bought more food—"

"Taken care of."

"Gotten gifts for everyone."

"Done."

"Chance," she said, laughing at the joy of having him there, "you make it really difficult to come up with reasons to panic."

"No need to panic, Stella. It's not your style. Now how about we open the door and let the crew in? It's cold out there tonight."

"Was that the doorbell?" Trinity called from the top

of the stairs, Beatrice beside her, her face beaming with happiness.

She looked beautiful and content and at peace, and Stella's heart filled with thankfulness that she'd survived, that they'd get to have Christmas together.

"Are they here?" Trinity continued. Chance opened the door, and a dozen people piled in. Men. Women. Kids. All of them smiling and laughing and chatting.

Stella was laughing, too, holding Chance's hand as he tugged her to the doorway that led into the parlor.

"What are you doing?" she asked. "You haven't introduced me to everyone."

"They know who you are," he responded, smiling as he pulled something from his pocket.

A box.

Pretty blue velvet.

Old.

He opened it, and the house went quiet.

Or maybe the sounds just faded away, because there was a ring inside. A pearl surrounded by emeralds and rubies. Dainty and delicate. Beautiful.

"Chance—" she said, her heart welling up, filling with all the things she'd thought she'd never have—love and family and forever. All the fear of losing, of hurting, of saying goodbye lost in the joy of having this moment with him.

"Christmas colors. For our first Christmas together," he said.

"It's beautiful."

"You're beautiful," he murmured, kissing her softly, the ring still in his hand. "I love you enough for forever, Stella. I can't imagine spending the rest of my life with anyone but you. Will you marry me?"

"She will!" Beatrice called, and Stella laughed through the tears that were filling her eyes.

Tears of happiness for this perfect moment.

This wonderful man.

Her life that had been filled with heartache, and was now filled just as full with love.

"I love you, too, Chance. And Beatrice is right," she said, levering up on her toes, kissing him deeply. "I will."

"Put the ring on her finger and let's get the show on the road," Trinity said, moving in next to them, grinning from ear to ear. "Christmas Eve service waits for no man."

Chance smiled, taking the ring from the box and sliding it onto Stella's finger. Sealing a deal that had been in the making from the moment they'd met.

"I'm thinking a winter wedding," he murmured, his hands on her waist.

"It is winter," she responded.

"I know." He grinned, taking her hand and leading her into the throng of people that were their family.

* * * * *

Don't miss these other MISSION: RESCUE *stories from Shirlee McCoy:*

PROTECTIVE INSTINCTS
HER CHRISTMAS GUARDIAN
EXIT STRATEGY
DEADLY CHRISTMAS SECRETS
MYSTERY CHILD

Find more great reads at www.LoveInspired.com.

Dear Reader,

Life is full of hardships. Some of us struggle with relationships. Some struggle with jobs, finances, health. I've been there this year, running from here to there, searching for some cure that will stabilize my health. One night, while I was lying in bed watching the moon rise outside the window, it occurred to me that I didn't have to rush and run and search. Everything I needed was already within reach. Maybe I would never have my health completely restored, but I had my family, my friends, my work and God. It was enough.

As I wrote Stella and Chance's story, I thought about that a lot. About how the things that we're running to and from aren't often the things we should be seeking. There is comfort in trusting in a God who is greater than our fear and our hardship and our troubles. I hope that you find that trust and that you hold onto it as you travel the path He has put you on.

I love to hear from readers. You can reach me at *shirlee@shirleemccoy.com* or find me on Facebook, Twitter or Instagram.

Blessings,
Shirlee McCoy

SPECIAL EXCERPT FROM

*When a CIA agent goes on the run home,
she'll need help from the local deputy to keep a
vulnerable young charge alive.*

Read on for a preview of
CLASSIFIED CHRISTMAS MISSION
by **Lynette Eason**, *the next exciting book in the*
WRANGLER'S CORNER *series!*

Deputy Lance Goode caught sight of headlights just
ahead on the sharp curve and slowed. He focused on
staying on his side of the road. The headlights came
closer. Followed by a second set. Who was crazy enough
to be out in this mess besides him?

He passed the first car and blinked. Even through the
falling snow, he'd caught a glimpse of the driver. Amber
Starke?

A loud crack split the quiet mountainside, and Lance
stepped on the brakes. Chills swept over him. He'd heard
that sound before. A gunshot.

When he looked back he saw Amber's SUV spin and
then plunge over the side of the mountain. The vehicle
behind her never stopped, just roared past.

Lance pulled to a stop. He headed to the edge to look
over. He saw the tracks disappear under an overhang.
Relief shot through him. Amber's sedan had only gone
down the slight slope, under the overhang, and wedged

itself between two trees. Now he just had to find out if the bullet had done any bodily damage.

He ran to his SUV and opened the back. He grabbed the hundred-foot-length rope that he always carried with him and hefted it over his shoulder. He lugged it to the front of the Ford and tied one end to the grill then tossed the rest down to Amber's car. It reached, but barely. With one more glance over his shoulder, he grasped hold of the rope and slipped and slid down the embankment to the car. He was able to duck under the overhang and squeeze himself between the rock and the driver's door.

Amber lay against the wheel, eyes closed. Fear shot through. *Please let her be all right.* He reached for the door handle and pulled it open. It hit the rock, but there was enough room for her to get out if she wasn't too badly hurt.

Amber lifted her head and he found himself staring down the barrel of a gun.

Don't miss
CLASSIFIED CHRISTMAS MISSION
by Lynette Eason, available wherever
Love Inspired® Suspense books and ebooks are sold.

www.LoveInspired.com

SPECIAL EXCERPT FROM

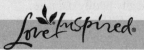
Love Inspired®

Could a Christmastime nanny position for the ranch foreman's son turn into a full-time new family for one Texas teacher?

Read on for a sneak preview of the third book in the **LONE STAR COWBOY LEAGUE: BOYS RANCH** *miniseries, THE NANNY'S TEXAS CHRISTMAS* by *Lee Tobin McClain*.

"Am I in trouble?" Logan asked, sniffling.

How did you discipline a kid when his whole life had just flashed before your eyes? Flint schooled his features into firmness. "One thing's for sure, tractors are going to be off-limits for a long time."

Logan just buried his head in Flint's shoulder.

As they all started walking again, Flint felt that delicate hand on his arm once more.

"You doing okay?" Lana Alvarez asked.

He shook his head. "I just got a few more gray hairs. I should've been watching him better."

"Maybe so," Marnie said. "But you can't, not with all the work you have at the ranch. So I think we can all agree—you need a babysitter for Logan." She stepped in front of Lana and Flint, causing them both to stop. "And the right person to do it is here. Miss Lana Alvarez."

"Oh, Flint doesn't want—"

"You've got time after school. And a Christmas vacation coming up." Marnie crossed her arms, looking determined. "Logan already loves you. You could help to keep him safe and happy."

Flint's desire to keep Lana at a distance tried to raise its head, but his worry about his son, his gratitude about Logan's safety, and the sheer terror he'd just been through, put his own concerns into perspective.

Logan took priority. And if Lana would agree to be Logan's nanny on a temporary basis, that would be best for Logan.

And Flint would tolerate her nearness. Somehow.

"Can she, Daddy?" Logan asked, his face eager.

He turned to Lana, who looked like she was facing a firing squad. "Can you?" he asked her.

"Please, Miss Alvarez?" Logan chimed in.

Lana drew in a breath and studied them both, and Flint could almost see the wheels turning in her brain.

He could see mixed feelings on her face, too. Fondness for Logan. Mistrust of Flint himself.

Maybe a little bit of… What was that hint of pain that wrinkled her forehead and darkened her eyes?

Flint felt like he was holding his breath.

Finally, Lana gave a definitive nod. "All right," she said. "We can try it. But I'm going to have some very definite rules for you, young man." She looked at Logan with mock sternness.

As they started walking toward the house again, Lana gave Flint a cool stare that made him think she might have some definite rules for him, too.

Don't miss
THE NANNY'S TEXAS CHRISTMAS
by Lee Tobin McClain, available December 2016
wherever Love Inspired® books and ebooks are sold.

www.LoveInspired.com